THE ONE FINAL RULE

AMBAR CORDOVA

Contents

Author's Note

Dear Reader,

I promised myself that my last Christmas novella, *The Gift Rarely Given*, would be my final rom com. I thought it was a fluke, a once in a lifetime story that popped into my brain when I needed it the most. And then…this project was born, and I was so excited to bring Mateo and Daisy's story to life. So I guess this is my way of saying 'never say never'.

If this is your first Ambar Cordova book, hi and welcome. I'm so happy you're here. Please know that most of my books are not rom coms like this one. If you're an Ambar Cordova stan and have read and loved my Baker Oaks series, hi and welcome. I'm so happy you're here. Please know this story is not angsty or emotionally devastating like my other books.

Now that that's out of the way, *The One Final Rule* is a contemporary romance Christmas novella set in The Dominican Republic and on Amelia Island, FL in beloved fictional places. It can be read as a complete standalone, but you might see some other characters pop up from *The Gift Rarely Given*. It is a novella, which means it's about half the length of a regular novel. It is meant to be a quick and fun story to read when life gets busy during the holidays.

I absolutely adore this story, and I hope you do too. Not only was it super fun to write, but it was absolutely incredible writing a Christmas novella in a tropical setting —said setting being my beautiful country, The Dominican Republic. Although this entire book (minus three chapters) takes place in the D.R., I wanted to note it takes place at a fictional resort, and the experiences of my characters are very much what tourists to the DR experience. It is not the reality of the whole country nor of the locals.

Also know that the Christmas Rules series features three other books by Latina authors all following the same timeline and the same setting. These are all standalones existing in a shared world, and you should absolutely go read those too!

I wanted to take a minute and acknowledge that although there are many celebrations during the winter season, this book particularly focuses on Christmas. I was but the vessel in telling Daisy and Mateo's story, and theirs just happens to be Christmas-focused. It also has some on-page topics that may cause discomfort for the reader. I will list them at the bottom of this page, as they may be spoilers, and I want to allow those of you who may not be sensitive to skip them if you wish.

This book also includes a playlist meant to be enjoyed per chapter to enhance the feels, but it can totally be read without it. Each chapter will tell you what song goes with it.

Now for the reader's content themes. There might be spoilers, so if you want to skip this next part of the author's note, you can. There will be profanity, on-page descriptions of explicit sex with slight kink exploration, PCOS, some descriptions of fatphobia, family drama, and some other woman drama.

Thank you again for giving this book a chance.

143,

Ambar.

Dedication

This one is for the boss babes. I hope you know you can be both an independent baddie and want to be called a good girl while you follow every one of the sweetie-pie-dirty-mouth-cinnamon roll's commands. Let Mateo Sanz remind you of that.

... and to everyone who calls me immature every single holiday season. I'm sorry you get zero daily good girls and need to be all grouchy and shit.

September & A Twatwaffle
SEPTEMBER BY EARTH, WIND AND FIRE

Daisy

"I'm on vacation, David. On. Vacation! Stop calling me, stop asking me to work, stop pretending I'm your damn assistant." I push the glass door open, letting the cool air of Fourth Street kiss my face as I look around the small deli.

"And actually, you probably shouldn't be calling him either. It's Labor Day. *Labor Day*. Take a day off. Leave me alone. Goodbye." I hang up the phone, sliding it into my bag and smiling softly at Mateo, who stands from his chair to greet me.

"Hi," he whispers, kissing my cheek as he always does and welcoming me into a warm hug. The effect this man has on me should be studied. One whispered hello, a hug, and half a kiss, and suddenly, nothing feels like a big deal anymore. My anger settles and I breathe easier. Always in his presence as if he was a calm down token.

"Sorry about that. I fucking hate him." I take a seat on

the little stool in the corner, my usual spot for our weekly deli dates.

"Why don't you just quit?" Mateo asks—as if it were that easy.

"Because I've had to work twice as hard as all those mediocre white men to get half as far, and I'm finally in a position I love. David, that motormouth twatwaffle, can go fuck himself."

He raises both hands in surrender, knowing damn well where I stand on this topic. It's already hard working in a male-dominated field, especially in the South. I finally got my dream job as event manager for The Eagles, the local baseball team, I'm not giving it up.

"I know, I know. I just hate seeing you this upset. But noted—your dream job, and you earned it." He smiles past me and waves at Ms. Kim, who is currently walking our way.

"Daisy, you're so beautiful today. What do you want to eat?"

"Thanks, Ms. Kim. You're always beautiful. The usual, please?" I ask, nodding and smiling at her and at Ms. Anna, who's standing behind the counter. Fourth Street Deli is a Korean family-owned deli on Amelia Island. It doesn't matter that Mateo and I live an hour away in Magnolia Springs; the food and the staff make it worth it to come all the way out here for lunch, even if it's only once a week.

"Also…hanging out with my sister much? Twatwaffle?" He chuckles, that deep, throaty sound reverberating through the quaint space and my damn body. It doesn't matter that I've known Mateo my whole life, friends since elementary school. The way my body reacts to him, like it's something new and exciting every single time, should be studied.

"Livie's bad influence is rubbing off on you," Mateo continues when I shrug, holding his bag of chips my way, offering to share while I wait for my food.

"I hang out with your sister as much as I usually do, thank you very much. But I do love her word choices all the time." Ms. Kim brings out our food, her face stretched in an *I love you like my grandchild* smile.

"I brought extra broccoli salad for you, Mateo. I know how much you like it." She pats Mateo's back after giving him an exaggerated wink, and I raise my eyebrow at him.

"Since when do you love broccoli salad that much?" I ask, lowering my voice and hoping a very sneaky Ms. Kim doesn't hear me. Yes, Mateo orders broccoli salad almost every time, but I end up eating it mostly on my own. This boy can eat a lot, but somehow, when we come here, he always leaves plenty left over. I've always wondered why he keeps ordering that particular salad if he won't eat it.

"I've always liked it. I just get full before I can eat it all and *you* steal it." I reach over with my fork, picking up a piece of the broccoli, and popping it into my mouth. I shrug and continue eating my food instead of his.

"I don't know who said a girl can't have it both ways— I get to order my favorite pasta salad and then still eat all your broccoli one. It's a win-win."

"You know I won't judge if you order an extra broccoli salad." He flashes his bright smile, and I lose my train of thought. I wish this feeling, the butterflies in my stomach when Mateo smiles at me, would disappear, but it never ends. It never goes away. He smiles at me, and everything stops, *all the time.*

"Why are we still talking about broccoli salad?" I ask, eager to change the topic.

"You love it, and I want to talk about all the things you love."

"Do you know what else I love?" I point my fork at him. "Rituals and routine."

"Oh, not again," he groans. He's referring to the temper tantrum I've been throwing over Mateo leaving me this Christmas to go with his family to the Dominican Republic.

"I just don't understand why you have to go. You don't want to, and I haven't spent Christmas Eve without you since…well, ever." My mom never really loved Christmas. She never liked any holiday, for that matter. She only celebrated Earth Day and our birthdays in the most bizarre ways: something relating to bees for my sister Bee, and something related to flowers for me. '*In honor of your namesakes*', she would say. So, when I met Mateo's family on the sidewalk after school, I asked if I could come. Mom shrugged her shoulders, and I've never spent Christmas Eve or Christmas without them.

I take a bite of my chicken salad sandwich, closing my eyes and trying to settle my breathing. The last thing I need is to sound clingy. Oh crap, I'm probably ovulating. That's why I'm so emotional and so…I don't know…sensitive. It always affects me so much— the hormone imbalance. It took me years to even figure out what was happening, but once I got the PCOS diagnosis, it made sense.

"I'm sorry, I—"

"You don't have to apologize, Daisy," Mateo interrupts. "But if you relax and take more than one breath per second, I can answer one of your questions." He offers me a sideways smile as he reaches over the table to hold my hand, drawing circles on the top. "I did try to get out of going, but my mother called to tell me Jaime is getting married."

I drop my food on the plate. "Jaime, as in your cousin Jaime?"

He nods.

"Jaime your cousin, the one dating the evil witch?"

"Daisy," he sighs.

"What? It's true. I hate her and she hates me, so I don't even feel bad about it." Violeta—Mateo's ex, who he proposed to two years ago, who said no and then started dating his cousin.

"She doesn't hate you." Mateo, the forever peace maker.

"She hated me. You can't lie about that. But back to the problem at hand... What did your mom say?"

He clears his throat. "Well, Jaime is getting married. He proposed last week, I believe. She said yes, and since the whole thing is a family reunion, they decided to get married there. Her uncle owns the resort or something."

"On Christmas?"

He nods.

"Your favorite holiday?" I ask.

"It's not."

"Why are you contradicting me on everything today, Teo? You fucking love Christmas." I take a sip of my drink and smile fondly at Ms. Kim and Ms. Anna, who look at us with concern. "You're not going, right?" This time, I whisper.

He lets out a breath while he traces his face with his hand. "I have to. I don't have a choice. It'll be miserable, but I'll be fine. I'm gonna miss you, though. First Christmas without you since we were, like, seven."

"You were seven. I was four, thank you very much. You're not going to miss me because I'm going." What? Sometimes I surprise myself with the shit that comes out of my mouth.

"You can't go."

"Are you telling me you don't want me to go?"

"No, not at all. I just…the tradition is that the only plus ones are spouses or significant others. I'm not gonna drag you to the Dominican Republic just to spend a bunch of time by yourself. I know how much you hate that."

He's not wrong. Even when I want quiet time, I like to be around him and our friends. I hate feeling alone, even if I'm not lonely. And I never feel alone when I'm with him.

"What if I come to the actual wedding too?" I take a sip of my sweet tea.

"I already told you, it has to be a spouse or significant other. It's ridiculous, but still, I can't just be like, oh yeah, I'm bringing Daisy as my plus one and we're dating now."

Aaaaand the sweet tea goes down the wrong pipe, making me cough.

Mateo's eyes go wide. "Are you okay?" He stands and pats my back as if I were a baby—like that's going to help.

"I'm fine." I clear my throat.

"I was kidding, obviously." He goes back to his seat, taking the last bite of his food.

I toss the idea around my head. Could it work? Could we pretend we're dating so we don't spend our holidays apart and so he doesn't have to go to the wedding from hell by himself? But what does Mateo want? His family never asks him. His job never asks him. He's never putting himself first, always trying to keep others happy instead.

"What do you want?" I ask.

"Right now? To not talk about my ex's wedding."

"I know, I know, but you have to. What do *you* want?" I press.

He thinks about it, searching my eyes. Maybe he's searching for answers, but I have none. I want him to tell me what *he* wants. He sighs. "To spend Christmas with my best friend, as usual."

"Okay, then look at me. You have two choices here.

You can take me with you and go to the wedding to make your mom happy…or you can just not go. Stand up to your mother and say fuck you all, bitches!"

"Daisy…" Mateo shakes his head.

"Miss Daisy!" Ms. Kim shouts from behind the deli case. She's always telling me to watch my language.

"Sorry, sorry. I got carried away." I shrug apologetically and look at my best friend, a smirk on his face.

I lower my voice. "Sorry. Anyway, you have choices here. Just make one."

"And what? Bring you and then leave you to spend the rehearsal, wedding, and the noche buena dinner by yourself?"

"No, silly. We pretend we're dating." This time, Mateo is the one practically choking.

"What do you mean?"

"You'll call Ms. Ada, tell her you're bringing a plus one, and we'll pretend we're dating each other. Easy peasy lemon squeezy." I sit back in my chair and cross my legs in victory.

"You can't be serious, Daze."

"I am one hundred percent serious. It won't be *that* hard. I already know you better than anyone else. It will be so much fun!" *Daisy, what are you thinking? It will be so much fun? Fake dating the man you've always loved?*

"You'd do that?" he asks, almost shyly. "It's such a big sacrifice. I don't want you to do this just to make sure I'm not alone."

"What's a big sacrifice? Spending time with you? Laughing with you? Going swimming with you? Things I do willingly all the time. Add doing all that in the Dominican Republic and pissing off Violeta? Sounds like child's play to me."

I should get an award for this performance. My words

carry a strength and steadiness that my heart doesn't share. I'm both giddy and terrified, but I can't let him know. If he finds out I'm nervous, he'll say no, and he'll be miserable watching that harpy twat marry his cousin.

He sits back, pushing his plate forward like it will hurt him, letting me steal the rest of his broccoli salad. He doesn't reply. He just sits and waits for something. Whatever it is, I don't want to overthink it, so I continue eating the salad like my heart isn't skipping beats in my chest.

"But also, Teo, you don't have to decide anything right now. Offer stands. You have four months to figure it out. Just keep me posted, yeah?"

He nods, gladly taking the change in conversation, waiting for me like he always does.

2

December & We're Not Married

'TIS THE DAMN SEASON BY TAYLOR SWIFT

Daisy

"Hello, my darling." I drag my bag out through my condo's front door. Mateo shakes his head and steps toward me quickly.

"Let me get that for you, Daze." He tries to run around me, and I huff. "It doesn't make you less independent to let me carry your bags for you. You can be a badass woman —" I cross my arms over my chest; he knows how hard I work to be perceived as exactly that. He raises his hands in defense "—like you already are, and let me carry your bag."

"I can do it." I all but pout, walking behind him since he ripped the suitcase from my hands.

"I know you can, but that doesn't mean you should." He walks ahead of me towards his SUV and tosses my bag in his open trunk. He offered to drive us to the airport, since it's about an hour away and we didn't both need to drive. His family is already in the Dominican, but because we didn't have a lot of time off, we're arriving today.

It took me weeks to convince Mateo to take me with him to this wedding. Eventually, it was his mom hovering, pushing him to accept the invitation from his girlfriend, who made it happen. He told her he was bringing a girl-friend but nothing else, that everything was new and he didn't want to jinx it, so nobody knows it's actually *me* going. It all makes me extremely nervous, because I've known his family just as long as I've known Mateo. It feels weird to lie to everyone, but at least it will be just for the weekend—right? We didn't talk that far about it.

"Hey, Teo?" I ask, looking out the window and admiring how beautiful the spring-fed lake looks with the soft colors of dawn cast over it.

"Mmhmm?" Though Mateo is a morning person, he doesn't talk much, so him answering with sounds is very on track for him.

"We need to talk logistics about this whole thing. We literally just agreed and rolled with it, but now the day is here, and we need to get our ducks in a row."

"I know." He lowers the volume to the music I didn't even notice was playing. "I figured we would tell them we've just been testing things out and we didn't want to make anyone uncomfortable."

Has he been thinking about this? He has, hasn't he? "Okay, sounds good. Your sister is gonna kill me though."

"Why?"

"Because we're gonna pretend in front of her that we're together, and then what? In four days, I'm gonna be like *juuuust kidding* and go back to being your best friend?"

He ponders my question, scratching his thick dark beard. The man has the best beard I've ever seen—that the world has ever seen, actually. He even won a contest once.

The summer I turned twenty one, we went on a cruise with our friends. Mateo, Holden, Lucas, and even Aspen, the youngest in the crew, all participated in as many contests as they could. Liam, the oldest, was the only one who sat out and stayed back with me. I wish he would have let himself relax a little, but instead, he continued to be his grumpy self, even if all of our friends and their beards participated in the most ridiculous contest to ever exist. Even Holden, who only has a mustache, participated. No one could hold a candle to Mateo, though.

"What if we just tell her and Alex?" Mateo asks, grounding me back into reality. "They won't say anything, and then she won't get her hopes up. We both know she's been trying forever to make this happen."

It's true. Livie has been saying all her life how she wishes I was legally her sister. She has tried to pair us together for so long. Mateo has never seen me as more than his best friend, and his friendship means the world to me. I can't mess it up by telling him my feelings. Half the time, I don't know if I'm in love with him or just completely infatuated. He's gorgeous, yes, but he also is the best friend I could ever ask for. Maybe what I really love is him as a person in general and not necessarily him romantically. Who am I fucking kidding, though? I've considered all the what ifs of what would happen if we were to be more than friends.

"Daze?" he asks, snapping me out of it.

"Sorry. Yes, that's not a bad idea. I would hate to lie to them." Livie got married this past summer to Alex, a former football player with a bad rep with the media. He's the perfect match for that firecracker of Mateo's sister. They met last Christmas, and by the summer, they were saying I do. I've never met two people more worthy of each other.

"I'm so excited they're going to be there, even though Livie will probably be busy spreading all her Christmas cheer."

"It's different there. Christmas is still lively and fun, but it's different. It's more about gathering. I think you'll like it," he adds.

"Good. That, and having Livie around will help with spending a few days with the evil witch."

He chuckles, looking my way with a smile. "Are you ever going to stop calling her that? She didn't do anything wrong."

"Stop defending her! She strung you along for so long and then said no when you proposed? Now she's marrying your cousin? Out of all the men in the world. I cannot believe her. Who would do that?"

"Daze," Mateo whispers.

"Sorry, rambling."

"You know you don't have to apologize, but you also don't have to fight my battles. It's fine. I'm not losing sleep over it."

He doesn't add anything else, but I get the feeling he still has something to say. Aaaaand now I know so, judging by the way he pinches his nose.

"What?"

"She's not the reason I didn't want to come," he replies, taking his eyes off the road for a second and looking at me.

What does he mean?

"Then what is?" His phone rings, interrupting the conversation. His boss' name flashes across the screen on the console. "Why is he calling you so early?"

"He always does. He must have forgotten I'm off today. Hold that thought."

Mateo clicks Accept Call on his steering wheel, and

Jason's voice inundates the vehicle. That man looooves to talk, so I know it'll be a while. I pull my current read out of my bag, along with the couple of highlighters that match the cover so I can annotate as we drive to the airport.

"It's beautiful here. I don't know how your parents ever wanted to move to the States. Look at the water."

"Now you see why I don't go to the beaches back home. I just wish I had time to come here more often." The road itself is exactly the same back home. It was ignorant of me to assume I was going to find dirt roads everywhere. I haven't traveled much outside of the United States, and when Mateo and Livie's family talked about the Dominican, I only imagined the beaches. I knew the beaches would be beautiful, but the luxury every building showcases is definitely mouth-dropping.

The driver pulls up to the entrance of a resort and the view is even better than I could've imagined.

I step out of the vehicle, trying to gather my bearings and my jaw, which had apparently decided to land somewhere near the pavement. Palm trees sway like they'd been rehearsing, in perfect synchrony; the air smells faintly of salt and new leather, and the lobby looks like it has been plucked straight from a Pinterest board.

"This way," Mateo adds, walking to the reception desk completely unfazed. He drags my suitcase with him through the marble entrance, and I have to speed-walk to catch up. He hands the bags to the bell boy and keeps walking.

"You said this was low-key," I whisper, trying to pull at his shirt.

"It is." His smirk is playful, and I'm swooning again. No, not swooning, Daisy. Focus.

"This is not lowkey," I mumble.

"Daisy Zimmerman, did you not do your research?" His eyes open wide in complete amazement. The reality is, I don't go anywhere unprepared. My plan Bs have a plan B, always. But work has been extremely difficult this season, and I didn't think much of this weekend. I figured, how hard could it be to show up to the Caribbean for a few days? Apparently, damn fucking hard if this is what it looks like everywhere.

"I'm wearing leggings and a hoodie, for Christ's sake," I whisper-shout, making him chuckle.

Well, great; there's that stupid laugh accompanied by that stupid dimple under the edge of his beard. Just one dimple, a non-dimple, according to him. He hit his cheek when he was six, right before I met him, and tore his muscle. Now, he has the most perfect dimple, because life's not fair.

"You look great, as usual. It'll be fine."

It's finally our turn to check in, and I take the time to let my hair out from the tiny ponytail it's been captive in all day. I remove my hoodie swiftly and slide it into my handbag. I perform what could be considered a small jump and stand next to him. As small as it can be, considering I'm a thick, tall girl.

He scans something around my face. *Oh, my hair.* "You like? I had an existential crisis, and it needed to go."

By existential crisis, I mean I couldn't fit in half my bathing suits since I've gained weight this past year— thanks PCOS for being a bitch. It's not that I don't love my new curves and rolls, but it's annoying how much my body changes without warning. I'm eating the same way and working out as often as I can, but with the damn hormonal imbalance and how sky high my cortisol levels are because of my job, I can't maintain my weight.

"You cut it all off," he whispers in a groggy tone, running his fingers through my hair.

I shrug and shake my head, letting my dark bob bounce near my shoulders. "Not *all*, silly, just about ten inches. Does it look bad?" It's not that I didn't expect a reaction from him, but more like I wasn't expecting this, whatever it is.

"Nothing looks bad on you, Daisy." See? This is why. This is why my stomach does little somersaults and my heart drops. Why does he have to say sweet things like this, with his husky tone and his glazy, dark chocolate eyes?

"Then why are you acting like this?" Mateo doesn't have a chance to answer, because the front desk agent interrupts our conversation.

"Here you go. Your key to your room, Mr. and Mrs. Sanz." I practically choke on my spit.

"She's not—"

"We're not—" we both say in unison.

I shake my head and smile. "Go ahead."

"We're not married, and it should be two rooms," Mateo adds.

She clicks the keys on her computer, and with concern on her face, she says, "I'm sorry, it says there is one room for Mateo Sanz with two adults in the room…" She continues talking, but her voice becomes a muffled sound. I have zero issues spending time with Mateo, but in the same room? There's no need to freak out, though; he'll fix it.

"Not a problem. Can I just pay for an additional room?" he asks.

"I can pay too." That earns me a narrow-eyed stare from Mateo. He's the easiest going person I know, but some things, he won't let go. Me paying for things is one of them. He never lets me, no matter how hard I try.

"I am so sorry, but we are fully booked. I only have this room available. I apologize for the inconvenience. I can check with our sister resort, if you'd like." The Splendor Resorts have more than one property in their chain, but this one, The Caribbean Splendor Resort, has the most perks. According to Mateo, that is, because I was just along for the ride and didn't read anything beyond it.

He looks at me with questions behind his dark brown eyes. "It's up to you, Daisy. I'll happily move to another location if that's what you want."

What *I* want? It shouldn't matter what I want. It should be about what's best for us. And staying in the same room should not be what's best.

"Mateo, you made it," a voice I would recognize anywhere says from behind us. We both turn to see his mom, Ada, walking toward us. She got here a few days ago, so where we look like traveling bums—at least I do— she looks refreshed, relaxed, and completely shocked to see me. *Oh shit.*

"Daisy?" she asks as soon as she kisses Mateo on the cheek. She often offers me the same greeting, but she doesn't this time. She's really thrown off by this. *Greeeeeat.* When Mateo said he wouldn't tell his mom who his plus one was, I thought it was a good idea. A lot of things seemed like a good idea four months ago. Not so much anymore.

"Hi, Mrs. Sanz. Good to see you."

"Likewise, sweetheart. Where are my manners?" She closes the space between us, kissing my cheek and smiling with a puzzled look.

"Mateo, I thought you said your girlfriend was coming."

"Mm-hmm. She did." He steps closer to me, his spicy, clean masculine scent wrapping around me as his large hand touches my lower back. I feel tiny next to him, and I love it. Considering that I'm five foot ten, it's rare that a man makes me feel small. Mateo, at well over six feet, does, and I love it. It makes me feel protected, always has, since the day he almost punched little Teddy in the face for calling me a boy on the bus. I didn't take offense to it, but Mateo did. He reminded that little punk that girls could play sports too, and if he tried to make fun of me again, he was going to show him. Little Teddy never bothered me again, and I'm pretty sure that's the day my self-esteem got the boost it needed. It allowed me to always be myself without worrying about what other people might think, because at least Mateo, one of the most important people in my life, had my back.

I smile at Ada with a nod. Her dark chocolate eyes, the ones that mirror Mateo's, travel between us, searching for the lie or the joke or something, but we stand our ground. *Deep breaths, Daisy, deep breaths.*

"You're dating Daisy?" she asks incredulously. Ouch. She, of course, likes me as a person, maybe as another daughter, but clearly not enough to be the perfect partner for her precious son. She's so harsh in her opinions of her kids' lives. Last Christmas, it was a whole thing with Livie. Ada made mean comments about Livie's weight in front of her now husband. Is she thinking the same about me? That I am somehow not good enough for Mateo because I'm thick? Because I'm me?

"I am, Mom. I didn't want to jinx anything, so I didn't tell you who it was. Yes, Daisy and I are finally giving this a chance. Aren't we, baby?" He places a soft kiss on the top of my head. A kiss that reaches all the way to my toes along with the goosebumps awakening my senses.

Oh damn. If I can't get my life together with one simple kiss on the head and a *baby*, what am I going to do if I have to kiss this man in front of people? On the lips? What if I have to kiss this man on the lips? *Oh my God.*

"Daze?" he asks, breaking me from my thoughts.

"Sorry, sorry. Yes, baby. We are. Sorry we didn't tell you." I don't dare to drop my gaze. I adore her, yes, but she won't make me feel any certain way about myself just because she doesn't approve. "But it's been…well, we're trying to figure this out first," I add.

"Oh, well, that's good." She holds my hands, fake-smiling at me. I can tell when it's genuine and when it's not. "I'm glad it's you then."

"I am so sorry to interrupt, but I need to know if you'd like me to call the other property." Oh shit, the room.

"Nope, no need. Here, I'll take the keys." I all but snatch the keys from the desk and smile at her.

"Thank you for all your help. Come on, baby. We have a busy day ahead," I say, holding Mateo's hand and pulling him away from the desk.

"We'll see you later, Mom."

"Adios, Mateo. See you later. There's a celebration at three by the pool. Don't forget."

"How could I? I'll be there." He stops and tucks me in his arms. "We'll be there," he adds. Mateo laces his fingers with mine, leading the way to our room.

We walk in silence, probably both pondering what just happened. *Trial by fire, that's what.* We need to lay some ground rules ASAP, or we won't make it unscathed.

The stone pathway is lined with birds of paradise, hibiscus, and some other plants I don't recognize, meandering between the beautiful terracotta and beige buildings. The place is stunning. The scent of salt drifts in from the ocean, carried on a lazy breeze kissing my cheeks.

We're far from where we started, but Mateo still doesn't drop my hand.

We turn onto a quiet path until we make it to the dark wood door with the number 1108 on it. Mateo slides the card in, the green light flashes, and he swings it open, allowing me to walk in.

Aaaand fuck my whole life. I drop his hand immediately at the sight. As if sleeping in the same room as this man wasn't enough, there's only one bed.

One bed.

One very large, very white, very smug-looking bed. Smug looking? Beds surely don't have feelings, but it one hundred percent looks smug right now. Right here, centered in the middle of the room like it knows it's about to cause trouble. Not even a 'two twins shoved together' situation, or two queens. Nah, this is an unapologetic king, dressed in crisp sheets and an aggressive number of decorative pillows. Taunting. Secretly wishing for our demise. One fucking bed.

I must be losing it. I'm having a whole ass conversation about a bed in my head. *Oh shit, Mateo.*

"Uh…this is…not what I—" My brain short-circuits, probably because I'm suddenly very aware of Mateo standing right behind me, his hand brushing my hip as he leans in to look.

"Looks like a suite. Maybe they thought we were newlyweds. She did call us Mr. and Mrs." I freeze at his words. I don't say anything. I just stand and gawk. I'm going to be sick.

"What a romantic getaway, I guess," Mateo adds.

I spin around, pointing an accusatory finger at him. "We are not doing the *romantic getaway joke*. There's nobody here to pretend in front of, Teo. What are we gonna do?"

Mateo steps further inside, tossing his backpack into

the corner of the room. "Daze, it's fine. I'll ask for a cot or something."

"Mateo you're a giant. You won't fit in a cot, and I'm too heavy for one. I'll break it."

"You're not too heavy," he breathes.

"For a cot, I sure am. You won't fit in one, and neither will I." I blink at him. "I'm calling the desk. There has to be another room."

"Then I'll make a bed with the pillows. It truly is not a big deal, Daisy. Take the bed. I'll be fine."

I narrow my eyes. "You'll be fine? Oh, sure. You, six-foot-three, all limbs and smugness, curled up on a decorative pillow pile like a princess' pet. Sounds perfectly comfortable."

"Five."

"What?" My hands land on my hips, exasperated by his chillness. Why is he so calm? Why is he always so calm? Nothing bothers him. Nothing phases him. He's always so put together—unlike me, with a complete storm inside my thoughts.

"I'm six-foot-five, not three." Mateo smirks, leaning on the wall like he's a comedian and it's a prop in his stand-up set. "You're picturing it now, aren't you?"

"Picturing what?" I ask, annoyed.

"Me trying to sleep on top of a bunch of pillows." He chuckles.

Unfortunately, I am.

Unfortunately, he's shirtless in that mental image for no reason.

I shake my head, trying to physically fling the thought out of my head. "Nope. Not doing this. I'm going to call the desk, and you're going to—" I point toward the balcony like I'm banishing him to sea, "go look at the ocean or something."

"She already said there wasn't another room. It's fine. I promise. It's not like we've never shared a bed before."

He's not wrong. We have. However, it was when we were tiny children, not full grown adults. It was back when the biggest conundrum was whether we would catch fireflies or gnats, not whether I'll be able to breathe sleeping next to the best friend I'm in love with.

"It's not the same," I whisper.

"Why?" He squares his shoulders and lifts an eyebrow, challenging my comment. I wiggle my toes and press my fingertips against each other nervously.

"We were children the last time we shared a bed."

"And, what? Now I'm the big bad wolf and you're afraid?"

"No, it's not that," I counter quickly. "I don't know. I'm just nervous, I guess, about the whole thing."

Mateo's expression softens as he walks up to me. He holds my hands and smiles. "Why are you nervous, Daisy? It's me. It's just me. It's us, just with an added layer. But if this is too much, we don't have to go through with it. It'll be fine."

Fine.

Fine.

Fine.

None of this is fine.

I search his eyes for a clue he's lying or upset, but I should know better. I should know that he wouldn't be upset at me for backing out now. He wouldn't, but I would. I can't do this to him. Not after we're here and we already lied to his mom. I should've thought more about this before I jumped to the *let's pretend to date each other* game. I should've thought about the consequences and what we would tell his parents after this trip is over. Now, it's too late.

One thing's for sure though: whatever this is and what-ever happens this weekend won't affect our friendship. We're more than that. If I've been able to hide my feelings for him all this time, I sure as hell can hide them during the trip.

"You're right. I have nothing to fear. It'll be fine. But don't be silly. You don't have to sleep on the floor. We're both adults, right?"

"Right," he answers quickly. *Exactly*. He doesn't look at me that way, so one bed is not as big a deal for him as it is for me.

"We'll put pillows in between us. At least the bed has a bazillion of them."

A knock rattles the door, and I spring back like I've been caught stealing cookies or something. *Perfect timing.* I smooth my hair, march over, and swing the door open. The bellman stands there, cheery and oblivious, a stack of our bags in tow. I step aside with exaggerated relief, allowing him in like he's a one-man cavalry sent to rescue me from the quicksand.

Saved by the bell. Literally.

3

Ridiculously, Hopelessly Stupid
DAMOCLES BY SLEEP TOKEN

Mateo

It's the way she froze when the desk clerk called us *Mr. and Mrs. Sanz*. The way her lips parted like she was about to protest, but I beat her to it. Or maybe we both did, I don't know. The world narrowed to just her—especially her freshly-cut hair. Damn, she looks good with it. But when doesn't Daisy look good?

I have to embrace my calm façade when I'm near her, because if not, she'll see how I truly feel about her. And it's stupid—ridiculously, hopelessly stupid—that a woman I've known most of my life can still make my stomach tighten just by saying my name. But there it is.

When my mom walked up? That was chaos.

When I wrapped my arm around Daisy's back? That was instinct.

When I kissed the top of her head and called her *baby*? That was...dangerous, especially how easy it came out, how easy it was to pretend she was mine. I've wanted this for so long. It's never a good time, though, not when a friendship like ours is at risk. In the meantime, I just keep bouncing the 'what ifs' in my head, replaying the never-ending scenarios of never being happy if I'm not with her.

Now, here we are, a few hours later, at the pool, waiting for everyone. They said three o'clock, but I should have known better. I should've known that meant four for them. If there's one thing I didn't pick up from my family, it's the impunctuality. Being late drives me absolutely wild. Nobody's here—at least nobody I recognize—but that's okay. I'm taking the time to relax. No phone, no work, for the first time in months. I'm thankful for the forced time away and for my Ray Bans. I'm thankful I can hide the fact that my eyes won't stop tracking Daisy.

She's reading a book she said was sad, but she needed to finish it. Something about World War II. I'm watching the sunlight hit the curve of her shoulder, relishing in the way it makes her hair look almost blue. Daisy has natural brown hair, but she dyes it black, has for as long as I can remember. Her little sister, Bee, does the same but with blonde. She's been a blonde since she could afford to pay for the hairstylist to do it.

Daisy has a swimsuit underneath the dress she's wearing, sunglasses framing her face. I'm lost in thought about seeing her in it. It wouldn't be the first time, since we go swimming often, but I always like seeing her body, even when she hasn't loved it herself. I always tried to remind her how powerful and beautiful her body is, even if it has changed through the years. We're supposed to—change, that is. And there's beauty in it. There's beauty in not looking eighteen anymore, in getting creases by your eyes from smiling so much. There's beauty in developing the sexiest and most alluring curves I've ever seen.

I can't stop thinking about the bed situation, and not in

the 'best friends at a sleepover' way. No, in the way I wish I'd get to touch her without holding back. I'd get to press my chest to her back and bury my face in her hair until I fell asleep breathing her in.

And yeah, that thought has to be shoved deep, deep down because she doesn't know. She can't.

I can't wreck this. I can't break our friendship over my feelings when I know she doesn't reciprocate them. She gets so jittery when I hold her gaze or when my eyes find her in a crowded room. She always smiles or pushes me out of the way, clearly indicating even that's too much. And that's just a gaze, not even a kiss. *A kiss*. We really need to talk about the rules of our arrangement.

"You look like you're plotting something," she says, bringing me back to reality.

I smirk. "Maybe I am."

And it's true—I'm plotting how to make it through the rest of this trip while letting every single person here see exactly how badly I want her but not letting *her* believe it's true. At the end of the day, we have to go back to our lives and pretend like nothing happened.

My comment earns me that skeptical little squint she does when she's deciding whether to press me for details.

She doesn't press. Instead, she pushes herself out of the chair and takes off her dress in one swoop. "I'm tired of waiting for your family. I'm getting in the pool. Wanna come?"

I shake my head. "I'll wait here. You go ahead."

"Suit yourself." She drops her dress over the book she left on the table and walks toward the water. "Make sure my book doesn't get wet, okay?"

The girl is always reading. I thought she may want to use her kindle on this trip, but no, she said paperbacks are for vacation.

She disappears into the water for what feels like an eternity, but eventually, she climbs back out. There's water cascading down her beautiful, long, thick legs, and I have to lean back in my chair like I'm trying to avoid the splash from some kids playing when in reality, I'm trying to hide the way my gaze lingers and my dick twitches.

She grabs her towel and drapes it over her shoulders, sits, and immediately starts wringing water from her hair. I shouldn't be staring at her fingers twisting through the dark strands and wishing they were mine instead. I shouldn't be thinking about how I could be the one doing that, slow and lazy, just to see if she'd shiver, how I wish I could rake my fingers through her hair and tug lightly at the bottom to give me better access to her mouth.

I clear my throat and glance toward the bar. "You want something to drink?"

"Lemonade," she says, leaning back in her chair. Her eyes close against the sun, a smile tugging at her mouth, like she's finally relaxed.

I'm halfway to the bar when I see them—my mom, my sister, a few cousins…and Jaime, spilling into the pool area with that big, loud, Sanz energy that can take over any space.

Shit.

When I turn back, Daisy's already seen them. She's sitting up, towel clutched around her shoulders as she watches them approach. I can tell she's bracing herself. I want to tell her she doesn't have to, that she can just be herself and I'll handle the rest. I want to remind her how much my family already loves her, that this is just a little bit different.

I slip back into the role—her boyfriend for the weekend —and slide a lemonade into her hand just as my mom reaches us.

"There you are," Mom says, giving that tight smile she gets when she's still figuring something out. Her gaze flits between us like she's testing the story we fed her earlier. "We saved you a spot near the cabana."

"Thanks, but we're good here," I say easily, setting my drink down and resting a hand on the back of Daisy's chair. I don't have to touch her, but I do. My fingers find her shoulder, warm from the sun, and I let them rest there. Just enough to make it look natural. Just enough to feel her under my hand. Judging by the goosebumps spreading over her back, she must be cold, so I grab my towel and drape it over her too.

My sister Livie joins in, teasing us. "You two look cozy. Guess it's true what Mom said."

"What's that?" Daisy asks, smiling, though it doesn't quite meet her eyes.

"That you're finally together," Livie says with a wink.

I laugh, leaning down toward Daisy so my lips are close enough for only her to hear. "We need to talk to her later."

She tilts her head toward me, just slightly. I catch the faintest whiff of sunscreen and chlorine, and for a second, I forget to breathe. She's breathtaking.

"What?" I ask when I miss whatever she was trying to say.

"I said we do, but for now, let's keep this story straight." Her tone is hushed, her words just for me.

It's not the story I'm worried about. It's the fact that pretending feels way too much like the thing I've wanted for years.

And with my whole family watching, I have to keep my hand exactly where it is when all I want to do is pull her closer and never let go.

Livie doesn't even give us a chance to answer before

she's pulling two chairs over, practically pinning us in with her enthusiasm.

"Come on, join the party," Daisy says, waving at Alex, Livie's husband, to join us too.

Livie plops onto the edge of Daisy's chair, forcing her to scoot closer to me. So close, her bare knee brushes mine. So close, I can feel the cool dampness of her skin against my leg. I shift automatically, draping my whole arm along the back of her chair. It's what a boyfriend would do, but really, it's just so I can keep touching her.

"So," Livie says, pointing between us, "who made the first move? You or him?"

"I'm dying to know," Jaime, my cousin, says. Jaime and I aren't really close. We grew up semi-close, but his family spent half the time traveling and living in between places, which made it harder to form a bond.

So imagine my surprise when he updated his status on socials to show he was in a relationship with my ex. Did he even know I dated Violeta? No, he didn't. A small part of me always wondered why I was wasting my time with her instead of chasing after who I truly wanted.

Daisy laughs, awkward but adorable. "Depends on what you consider a first move."

"Her," I say.

At the same time, she says, "Definitely him." Damn it, we need to get on the same page.

Everyone laughs like it's the cutest thing in the world, and Daisy hides behind her lemonade glass, sipping to avoid the follow-up questions. I don't blame her.

I lean in just enough so only she can hear again. "We're supposed to get our stories straight, remember?"

She side-eyes me over the rim of her glass. "Okay, okay, sorry. Sorry. I'll hush now."

My chest tightens. I don't want her to be quiet. No, I

want to be on the same page as her while simultaneously trying to gauge if this is something she can do past this weekend.

"Mateo, help me with this umbrella," my uncle calls from behind us.

I start to move, but Daisy's hand lightly grips my thigh to stop me. "Stay," she says, her voice laced with concerned. My entire body goes still under her touch, just like it always does. I look at her with questioning eyes.

"I don't know what to say," she whispers.

I lean in closer, holding her neck with one hand and brushing her hair out of the way with the other.

"Play pretend. Just keep notes in your beautiful brain so you can share with me later." I kiss her forehead and walk to the other table to help my uncle.

By the time I wrestle the umbrella into place, more of my family members have gathered. Some are further away in the cabana where my mom is, others spread around the pool area.

The resort's pool deck is all gleaming white stone and low, airy cabanas with straw roofs. I look over to see Daisy tense. Her body language speaks volumes. Her gaze darts toward the cool blue sweep of the pool, the rows of sun loungers, then back to someone walking her way. Her shoulders are tense, her eyes narrowed, and she uses her drink as a shield.

Then, I see why.

"Well isn't *this* cozy." Violeta's tone is all sugared venom and razor edges.

"Violeta," I say, walking back toward Daisy to sit. Maybe my presence will keep Violeta from saying something hurtful. She looks exactly the same as the last time I saw her, and somehow, not at the same time. Her hair is longer than I remember, her sunglasses oversized, her smile as calculated as always. Her cheeks are plumper, and she has a different shine to her. She's happy. I'm glad she finally found what she was looking for.

Beside her, Jaime looks like he's trying to play peacemaker, but the smug tilt of his lips says he's enjoying this too much.

"Hi, Violeta," Daisy says evenly, forcing my jaw to unclench. Violeta is not Daisy's favorite person; she always had issues with Daisy for some reason. It got so overwhelmingly bad, I refused to let her talk about Daisy at all. It's one of the reasons why I knew it wouldn't work between us, even if I didn't have my own motives hiding in plain sight.

Her gaze flicks from me to Daisy, pausing deliberately on where my arm rests along the back of her chair. She takes in the towels, the easy way Daisy's bare knee still brushes my leg, and she smiles wider, like she's just found the punchline to a joke no one else is in on.

"So I was right," she says, voice honeyed, like the words are a compliment instead of a grenade.

Daisy straightens slightly, but her expression stays calm. "About what?" she asks, offering a polite smile that doesn't reach her eyes.

"You and Mateo ending up together," Violeta continues, eyes sliding back to me. "I could tell there was more going on…" She lets the sentence trail off.

I'm already opening my mouth to shut her down when Daisy speaks first.

"Well," Daisy says lightly, "I don't know what you think you knew, but Mateo and I didn't start dating until recently. Not that it's any of your business, though, considering you two are not a thing and haven't been for a while. You're getting married the day after tomorrow, right? So why does it bother you?"

It's not subtle at all, but just by listening to Daisy, with her sure tone and her eyes holding Violeta's, you could miss how she truly feels. There's steel under her voice. She's lightly pinching my thigh. She hates this—she just won't let her say some bullshit.

Violeta's eyes narrow just a fraction, but she recovers quickly. "Of course," she says. "We're happy you're here."

I lean forward, resting my elbows on my knees, making sure Violeta sees exactly how close I am to Daisy. "We're happy to be here too. Congratulations to both of you."

Jaime coughs into his drink, badly hiding a laugh. Livie, who's been half-watching from her spot, suddenly bounces to her feet.

"Okay," she says brightly, clapping her hands once. "I think Daisy and I are overdue for some sister-in-law bonding time."

Daisy blinks. "Sister-in-law?"

Livie grins, grabbing Daisy's hand and tugging her up before she can protest. "Future sister-in-law, same thing. Come on. I'm stealing you."

"Have fun," I call after them, ignoring the way Violeta's smirk sharpens. I sit back in my chair and ignore the rest of them for the time being.

4

Are You In Love With My Brother?

FIRST LOVE BY SABRINA CARPENTER

Daisy

"What the hell is going on?" Livie asks as soon as we're out of ears' reach.

I cross my arms over my chest and look down at her. For someone who has a tall brother, she sure as hell is a short little thing. Livie takes after their mother while Mateo is the spitting image of their dad, just younger and hot, obviously. Damn it, why am I thinking about this?

"Nothing is going on."

"Don't give me any of that bullshit. Tell me right now. You're uncomfortable, that's clear. You and Mateo are weird around each other, almost like all the chemistry you two have is out the window. I've never seen you so tense… like ever."

I look around—there's nobody around, just the palm trees framing the small stone path and the faint sound of people. "We were gonna tell you either way—"

"Are you pregnant?" Livie's face lights up with enthusiasm.

"What? No!" I shake my head and take a deep breath. "No, it's not that. We're just not a thing."

"Who's not a thing?" she asks.

"Me and your brother…we're fake dating."

Livie laughs. *She laughs.* Like folded over on herself laughs. When I don't respond in the same manner, she freezes and raises her eyebrows.

"Oh, you're not lying." I shake my head.

"Daisy!" Her eyes open wide.

"I know, I know." I let out a breath. "But you know how your mom is, how Mateo is, and, well, it seemed like a good idea at the time. Now, I'm not too sure." I bite my lip and watch her ponder something.

"Okay, I'm about to tell you something I haven't told anyone. I need us to sit down first, though. Come." She continues walking, this time towards the beach. After we checked in and went to the room, we went straight to the pool, so I hadn't touched the sand yet. This sand, though? It's white, almost like powder, and soft. It's not sticky and one hundred percent makes the contrast with the clear water seem even more drastic. It's so different from the beaches in Florida, even in the panhandle area. It's stunning. Livie sits on an empty lounge chair, and as soon as I do the same, she lifts her glasses to rest on her hair with a smile.

"Alex and I fake dated last year." There's zero hesitation in her words. It's a fact, one she's sharing it with me. Plain and simple, but it's hard to believe her—Alex and her are completely made for each other.

"What do you mean?"

"It's a long story, but for similar reasons as you and Mateo. I was tired of Mom asking me to bring a date or to get married or whatever. We hooked up, and after that, we agreed to help each other."

I'm sure if my eyes get any wider, they'd pop out of my face. "There's no way. You two are perfect for each other."

She chuckles. "We are. We truly are, but in reality, everything started with us pretending. Looking back, we should've just dated from day one. We had this insane chemistry and connection, you know? But hindsight is a privilege, and I see it clearly now. Which is why I wanted to ask you this… Are you in love with my brother?"

"Livie!" I shout.

"I'm not beating around the bush here, Daisy. We have no time, we need to get back to the wedding celebrations, and we both know my mother is gonna call for us soon. So, are you or are you not in love with my brother?"

What am I supposed to do here? Am I supposed to tell her the truth? A truth I've never told anyone, not even my sister? A truth I surely can't tell my best friends, considering all of them are also best friends with Mateo? Hell, Mateo *is* my best friend.

"Okaaay, so the silence is telling. Before you say something let me just add, I know you are in love with him. I've known practically all our lives. It's why I keep pushing you both to get together. For a second there, I thought maybe it was all in my head, but the timing of you both being single was a little too coincidental."

Busted.

"It wasn't like that," I add, and she lifts her brows in question. I shake my head. "Is it that obvious?"

This time, Livie is the one shaking her head. "No, it's not. I also grew up around you, remember? I know you so well. Daisy and I see the way you look at him."

"Oh please, do tell."

"Like he invented hot water."

"Livie!"

"It's true! What I don't understand is why don't you just tell him?" she asks as she holds my hand and smiles softly, offering me her sympathy.

"What Mateo and I have is rare. We have such a beautiful friendship, one we've had for years. I don't want to mess that up over feelings he doesn't reciprocate."

"What if he feels the same way?" she asks.

I shake my head and scoff. "He doesn't. He's dated so many girls, and none of them look like me. They're all short, blonde, and obnoxious. Well, except for Violeta."

"She's plenty obnoxious," Livie laughs.

"I meant blonde. She's not blonde." Mateo has a type. Pretty, short blondes with a light and bubbly personality. He doesn't date tall women with dark hair and curves for days. He doesn't date women who played sports for years and work in an unglamorous field. It has never made sense to me, though. He's so down to Earth. He'd rather spend a day couch surfing and in pajamas than going out to lavish parties. However, most of the women he dates are the complete opposite. Maybe that's why they don't last. Too incompatible.

"She's not, but she was also not right for him. I'm so happy he saw right through that."

He didn't, though. She did. She called it off. He proposed, and she said no. He was miserable for weeks. "What do you mean?"

Livie waits, pondering what to say, clearly holding something back. Well, that's new. Livie never holds anything back.

"Livie, what is it?"

"There you are. We've been looking for you." We turn to see Ada standing nearby. *Oh, great.* there's no way we'll finish up the conversation now.

"Sorry, Ma. I had to talk to Daisy before the rest of you swarm her. I've been waiting for this girl to be my sister all my life." Livie turns my way and winks at me. *Thank you, sweet angel. Thank you.*

"Don't spook the girl," her mom adds. "You need to head back. The games are about to start."

"Games?"

"So many games. It's part of the tradition. Come on." Ada walks ahead of us, and we follow, allowing some space between us so we can breathe. So I can breathe.

"Just do me a favor," Livie whispers.

"Yeah?"

"Be careful. I don't want you to get hurt. The line between pretend and reality can get blurry sometimes, and if you need me, I'm here." She holds my hand and squeezes it, smiling softly.

"Will do," I reply, squeezing back.

We make it back to where chairs and tables are set up near the bar and pool. These people have zero issues claiming all this space while the resort is buzzing with other guests. Mateo smiles as soon as he sees me, and I let go of Livie's hand.

He pulls me into his arms, engulfing me in his spicy scent, wrapping me up in him and completely messing me up for anyone else. "Everything okay?" he asks with a low voice.

"Mm-hmm. She knows," I whisper.

"Good. Now let's make sure nobody else does." He kisses the top of my head as we turn to face Jaime.

Poking The Bear

GIRLFRIEND BY AVRIL LAVIGNE FT.
LIL MAMA

Mateo

We've been playing games for the past two hours, and if
there's one thing you can count on with the Sanz family,
it's that we take competition way too seriously. Nothing
says family reunion like shouting, competition, and at least
three aunts threatening to disown whoever starts flipping
game boards.

We've done trivia. We've done a relay race that left my
little cousins crying, and now they've gone to take a nap.
We've done tug-of-war, charades, and even a dancing
competition with the resorts staff's help. When Mom said
we were picking this resort for our family reunion and that
Violeta's uncle owned it, I didn't think we'd have any
excitement—that girl is the opposite of fun—but it's been
amazing. Now, it's time for the finale: volleyball. One last
game before we scatter until dinner.

My dad has ten siblings; they all live in different parts
of the world, and they all have kids of different ages. Jaime

and I are the oldest cousins, so naturally, we get to be captains. I've been waiting for this all afternoon—not just because I like winning, but because I know exactly who I want on my team.

My girl.

No. Not my girl. What am I thinking? She's not mine. Not only do I not trust Violeta with Daisy, but Daisy is an athletic powerhouse. She was involved in all the sports our town offered growing up and excelled at all of them, volleyball being one of them. I'm sure she still owns it. But more than that, she loves it. I would give what I don't have to make sure she's having a good time.

So yeah. My first pick is obvious.

My dad steps forward with the coin for the toss.

"Heads," I call before the coin even leaves his hand. It spins, glints, and lands in the sand. My dad snatches it, peeks, and grins.

"Dale, mi hijo," he says, smiling like he's just made my whole year. "You go first."

I leap up, arms in the air like I just won the lottery. "Daisy," I say immediately, no hesitation, not even blinking.

Violeta grunts and crosses her arms. "Seriously?" She's been dripping venom since we started playing today, but somehow, she finds a new level of irritation just for this moment. "You've had her on your team for everything."

I smirk. "What can I say? I like to win."

Violeta narrows her eyes at me, her glare sharp enough to cut glass. Every time I so much as look at Daisy, Violeta acts like I've broken some sacred rule. Which makes zero sense, considering she's about to marry someone else, and I don't love her. I don't, and I never did. But by the time I realized that, it was too deep into our relationship.

From the sidelines, Livie rolls her eyes so hard, I'm

afraid they'll get stuck. "God forbid her boyfriend wants to spend time with her," she mutters, loud enough for everyone to hear. "Alright, let's go! We don't have all day!" Livie shouts, and everyone chuckles.

I glance at Daisy, standing a little apart, arms folded loosely over her chest. Maybe I imagine it, but it looks like her cheeks flush just slightly when she realizes I picked her first.

She walks over, bumping my shoulder lightly. "You didn't have to pick me first just because we're pretending to date," she teases, but there's slight hesitation in her voice that makes me wonder why she would think my priorities would shift just because we're pretending.

"I'll always be your number one fan, and you'll always be my top choice, Daisy girl."

Her cheeks flush a deeper color red, but I have no time to question it. I can't believe I called her *that*. It's my turn to pick again.

We split into teams quickly. Jaime grabbed Violeta as his first pick, and soon after, we're evenly split. I honestly don't care who else is on my team. I already got Daisy; the rest is just filler.

When we line up on the sand court, I sneak a glance at her. She's tying her hair back in a tiny ponytail, half of her hair coming loose and falling against her face. She looks… ridiculous. Ridiculously *good*. Ridiculously distracting. And I'm supposed to focus on winning this game? Good luck to me.

"Eyes on the ball," she says, catching me staring.

I cough, pretend to stretch, try to look casual. "That's exactly what I was doing."

"Uh-huh." She smirks, clearly not buying it.

Tio Carlos shouts, "¡Vamos!" Jaime serves first, and the game is on.

From the start, Daisy dominates. She moves like the court belongs to her, diving for saves, not caring one bit about being covered in sand, setting up perfect passes, spiking like she's trying to send the ball into orbit. Every time she scores, I want to cheer louder than everyone else combined, but I settle for a fist bump and a grin I can't seem to hide. A couple high fives later, and my girl is on fire.

At one point, she makes an impossible save—sliding across the sand, popping the ball up just enough for me to smash it over the net—and when we get the point, she jumps up and throws her arms around me.

It's less than the blink of an eye, but her body is pressed against mine, and my brain short-circuits. Focus. Volleyball. Game. Ball. Net. Family watching. *Family watching.* She's just pretending. I can do the same, though.

I pick her up by her round ass, forcing her to wrap her legs around me as I kiss her nose. Maybe I've been thinking about this situation wrong, and instead of worrying about Daisy realizing how I feel, maybe I get to show her how good we can be together.

Once our foreheads are close and nobody else can see I'm actually not kissing her, I say, "Nice save."

Her eyes sparkle, like she knows exactly how rattled I am. "Put me down, Teo. I'm heavy as shit."

"Nah, not for me. For me, you're just right." I keep my voice steady, even if she makes fun of it. I want her to know I mean it.

"Alright, love birds, let's gooooo!" my sister shouts, breaking the spell. I put Daisy down, smacking her barely-covered ass when she turns to walk to her middle blocker. She yelps and walks just a little faster.

The score's tight. Jaime's team fights hard, and Violeta keeps aiming serves directly at Daisy, like she's trying to sabotage her. But Daisy? She thrives under pressure. Every time Violeta targets her, Daisy just returns the ball with even more fire.

By the time we're tied at match point, the tension is heavy. Everyone's yelling; half the family is standing, the other half pretending they don't care but watching anyway.

The ball comes to my cousin Alexa, who sends it my way. I set it high, aiming for Daisy. She leaps, time slowing for just a second, her body suspended like it was designed for this moment. Then, she spikes it right to Violeta—except Violeta hesitates and moves over, as if the ball is heading out of bounds, but when she turns around, she sees what we all see. It landed right by the back line, cradled in a small dent in the sand, in bounds.

Point. Game. Match.

Our side erupts in cheers, but all I can see is Daisy, flushed and grinning, glowing with adrenaline, her eyes on Violeta. She turns to me, and before I can stop myself, I scoop her up, spinning her around.

She laughs, breathless, her hands gripping my shoulders. "Put me down!"

"Never," I tease, spinning until I trip and fall, landing on my back with Daisy on top of me. I open my eyes and find hers shut tight. "Are you okay?" I brush her silky hair from her face.

"I told you I was too heavy," she adds.

I chuckle. "You're not. I'm clumsy." My pause is deliberate so I can take this whole moment in. "We won. You did it."

"We did it. We're a good team."

"We are—we always have been."

She nods and lowers her head to my shoulder. "Sorry I fell on you."

"Daze, you didn't. I tripped, and I didn't want you to get hurt. I'll protect you. Always."

"Aren't they adorable?" Livie asks, breaking the spell— again. She's absolutely poking the bear.

"Come on, let's get rid of all this sand." I help her up, and in no time, we're walking to our hotel room with instructions to be back for dinner with the whole family at eight.

6

Rule Number One
UNCOVER BY ZARA LARSSON

Daisy

"I thought you weren't working on this trip," I say as I step out of the bathroom into the bedroom. Mateo is sitting on the bed with his laptop open on his lap, but his eyes lift slowly—deliberately—starting at my feet and dragging upward, unhurried, like he's savoring every inch of me.

I know what he sees: the one piece romper with wide-legged floral palazzo pants, the cut-out at my stomach, the bralette-style top that frames my chest. My outfit makes me feel confident, feminine, alive, but under Mateo's gaze, it suddenly feels…I don't know. Wrong? His stare lingers too long, burning into me.

"What's wrong?" The words tumble out before I even think. His eyes snap up to mine, dark and unreadable yet charged with something I've never seen before, something that coils low in my belly. I swallow hard. "I can change if this isn't…appropriate."

He says nothing. He just looks at me, the silence speaking louder than any other word. Fine. Noted. I spin on my heel toward the closet, but his hand catches my wrist.

"Daisy."

The single word makes my pulse stutter. When I turn, he's closer than I expected, his black linen pants hanging low on his hips, his shirt open just enough to reveal the gleam of the small gold chain he never takes off. God help me, it's unfair how good he looks. My mouth goes dry.

"Daisy," he whispers again, and my name has never sounded edged with hunger before.

"Wh—what?" My voice cracks, and his smirk tells me he noticed. "Why are you so smug?" I ask.

"You were checking me out."

"I was not!" My protest comes out too loud, too fast. My cheeks blaze with heat, and his smirk widens. Busted.

"It's okay, Daisy girl. You don't look so bad yourself." His voice softens, laced with something intimate, maybe even passionate. "Don't change. You look beautiful."

The sincerity in his tone sinks into me like warm tea after a long day of work. Mateo never shies away from giving compliments, but this one feels different—playful, yes, but also, I don't know…sexy?

"Daisy girl?" I echo. It's the second time he's used it, and, God help me, I want to hear it again.

"Trying to find something else to call you," he says, stepping closer, his presence erasing the space between us. "You didn't like it when I called you baby earlier. You froze. I want to be respectful."

Always so considerate. *Too* considerate.

"It just caught me off guard, that's all." Of course he just wants to make it seem real. He's not actually thinking about me in that manner.

"What did?" His voice is quiet now. He's too close, and I have to tip my head back just to meet his eyes. His cologne wraps around me, a dizzying scent. There's something about, I don't know, pretending we're together, him looking like this, my real feelings for him enhancing absolutely everything to the point of delusion.

"You calling me baby." The words scrape from my throat, broken and almost needy. Damn it, Daisy, get it together.

He lifts a hand, and I stop breathing. His fingers graze my cheek before tracing slowly over my lips, lingering there, teasing the corner of my mouth before pulling away. The loss is instant, leaving me agonizingly cold after warming me with just that single touch.

"Sorry," he murmurs. "Reflex. You had lipstick there."

"Oh." I touch the spot where his thumb was, where his touch still burns phantom-hot. My heart is racing, but I shake it off and breathe. *Breathe, Daisy. Breathe. You have to.* "Sorry. Are we ready?"

"Yeah, but…we need to talk. We need some ground rules. I don't know what I'm allowed to do with this. With us."

"What do you mean?"

"In this fake relationship…" His eyes lock on mine, searching. "I don't know where the line is. What I can do and what I shouldn't. I touched you so much earlier; is that okay? Like…what is actually allowed here?" I'm *so* glad he noticed how much he touched me. I was spiraling the entire time, but damn if I didn't like it. He probably had to force it. He probably needs to know ahead of time if he needs to touch me because it won't come natural to him, no matter how much it seems like it is.

His eyes show me so much concern. Concern and love. I know he loves me. He always has. As his best friend. The love one has for a sibling.

"Rule number one: don't lie to me." Come on, Daisy.

You can do this. Keep your feelings inside and set strict rules to protect yourself.

"Rule number two: No matter what, we're still best friends. Rule number three…we listen to each other." I smile with my eyes at him. I need him to know I'll be here no matter what, that I'm still his best friend.

"You know me. I know you. I trust you won't push me somewhere I don't want to go. And I won't either. Deal?"

I can't tell him oh *yeah and one final rule: I won't tell you how much I love you, how much I wish I was the woman for you.* I can't have a talk with him right now about whether he should or shouldn't kiss me. All I would want to tell him is to please not kiss me so my poor heart doesn't break more from the unrequited love. At least these ground rules seem straight forward; we don't have to add any more.

He studies me for far too long, but he finally nods once. "Deal."

7

I Might Have To Say Fuck The Rules
CAN I BE HIM BY JAMES ARTHUR

Mateo

I can't blame anyone who can't take their eyes off Daisy, because neither can I. She's stunning. Breathtakingly so. She always is, but tonight? Tonight, it's even more evident. It's not only the outfit she's wearing that was made for her body, but her tanned cheeks are making her almond-shaped, dark green eyes look glossy. Beautiful. So beautiful.

We had dinner, and it went without a hiccup. Being with Daisy has never been hard, so that was not the surprise. The surprise for me has been how easily we've fallen into this fake couple thing. My hand reaches for her often, or her knees seek mine under the table; even if nobody can see, she lets me, and I play pretend with my heart that this is real.

Right now, though, she's laughing at something Livie and my cousin, Tere, are saying. She's folded over, drink in hand, laughing. Her laugh carries over, above all the other noise, drowning everything into the background. There's not enough money in the world to buy something as perfect and as precious as her laugh.

"That feeling never gets old," Alex, my brother-in-law, says, low enough for only me to hear.

"What feeling?" I could be talking to the entire bar, and I wouldn't know, considering that my eyes are glued to Daisy and not paying attention to anything else.

"Like your heart will leap out of your chest at any given moment, or that it will stop if she stops laughing." That does it. That disrupts my staring, and I turn, raising an eyebrow at him.

"It's the way I feel about your sister. How long have you known you wanted to be more than friends?"

I don't know if Livie told him about our fake dating deal or what, but it wouldn't change my answer, so I play along and answer. "Honestly? Since she was a sophomore in high school and cried in my lap over a boy who wouldn't love her back. She kept rambling on and on about how the guy picked a girl because she was prettier and slimmer. I was more upset about her not under-standing that nobody was more beautiful than her than anything. I knew then."

She was so upset and kept crying, using all these self-deprecating words, words she had heard from other kids for years. I was so tired of hearing them. I just held her and reminded her of everything she is, including beautiful. Eventually, she just laughed it off and told me I was a good friend. No matter how many hints I left, she always laughed it off as if I was joking.

Friend zoned from day one. I got it and have never tried to cross that line again. Here, though? This is not only tempting but also scary, because I can see us doing this all the time. If she'd let me, I could show her how well

I could love her. If she'd let me, I could be everything she needs and more.

"Can I ask why it took you so long to take the step?" I ponder his question, letting it ping pong in my brain. Another thing we didn't talk about. We're flying blind here, and I don't know how to feel about it at all.

"It seemed like the planets finally aligned." Not a lie. Not completely, at least. It will never be the right time to tell your best friend you'd like to be more, not when everything we've built as friends is at risk. But this way, she can have a taste of it, and later, she might be able to just take the jump with me and give this a try.

The music changes from a merengue to a bachata. A bachata I love. Apparently, a lot of people in the resort love it too, because suddenly, the dance floor is full. It's the perfect opportunity to get away from this conversation; I don't know what Livie told Alex, and I want to pick Daisy's brain.

"I'll be back," I tell Alex, standing and walking toward Daisy. She's in the middle of a laugh, but when she notices movement, her eyes shift until they find mine. I smile, and she returns it instantly, mirroring my comfort like she always has. My entire body feels safe around her—my heart and my soul too. *Do you feel the same, Daisy? Does your heart mirror mine?*

The soft guitar strings carry the melody of a sensual song that reverberates across the floor. Tall chandeliers hang with colorful guirnaldas. Most people back home relate Christmas with snow, even in Florida, but this place doesn't. They're not taking things that don't belong on this island and using them for aesthetics. They use conches and shells to decorate the tree, poinsettias adorning corners and doors, and even sand as filler in a lot of bouquets and centerpieces. It's both tropical and Christmasy, a perfect juxtaposition to those who don't know the cultural meaning but absolutely perfect to those who can appreciate it.

With Daisy's hand in mine, we walk toward the dance floor silently, joining the couples who follow the perfect rhythm to the dance. This particular Aventura song is slow, and the closer you are to your person, the better it matches the meaning the song carries. The whole room oozes passion and intimacy. I should've thought about that before I asked her to dance this particular one with me, but it's too late now.

She swivels around, following my lead, and lands in my embrace, her hands on my chest. She's stiff, and I don't even understand why. "Relax for me, Daze," I whisper in her ear, making her visibly stiffen more.

"I don't know how to dance to this one particularly. I didn't want to say no, but I don't want to make a fool of myself," she replies, raising her eyes to meet mine. Those beautiful eyes are full of fear.

"It's the same as we've always danced, just closer. We're both adults, right?" She nods. "I've got you, remember? Always, no matter what." I hold her right hand, lifting it slightly while my other one drags down her back and rests right above the curve of her ass. I need to keep my half-hard dick as far away as possible, or I will have a lot of explaining to do. I take a deep breath, filling my lungs with flowers and joy, filling my lungs with her, letting it out and hoping with it, I gain some comfort.

"How was your evening?" I ask. Sometimes, small talk is the best medicine when you have your best friend in your arms and you can't touch her the way you've always wanted. You can't kiss her the way you've dreamed. You can't tell her all the things you wish you could.

She sighs and smiles. "Actually…I had fun. I love Livie,

but I didn't know your other cousins would be so similar to her. I'm having a really good time, even if that evil witch is around."

I chuckle. "You've got to stop calling her that before someone else hears you."

"I really don't care, Teo. She is, and she was acting even more like it all day. I don't understand what her issue is." I spin her around and back into my arms, but she gets lost in the steps. She looks at me with fear in her eyes, but when I shake my head and smile, she does what she always does and softens in my arms. Why is it this way with the only girl I can't have?

"She's just jealous, and there's nothing you can do to fix it. It's an insecurity she carries deep within her, and no matter what you may say or do, it won't change."

The song makes it to the slowest part, the part when often you pull your partner even closer. Pelvis with pelvis, torsos flush, hair on my shoulder—sex with clothes on, as my friends describe it. As close as Daisy is to me, I can't let her feel what she does to me, so I angle myself away, keeping my hard on hidden from her.

"Jealous of what?"

Her breath catches when my lips get close to her ear, and I whisper, "Of you." *Like every other woman in my life*, I want to say, but I don't. It's not her fault they can all sense that even if I wanted to give them my heart, it really, truly, only beats for Daisy.

"There's zero reason for anyone to be jealous of me. You and I are just friends, Mateo." *I know, but I want to change that.*

"Besides, she's about to get married, like in two days." Her words are anything but steady. Her breath is shallower the longer we stay this close. It's dizzying having all of her so close. Her hair, her body, her floral scent that accompanies her everywhere, her skin…

"Just trust me on this one," I say, stepping back and making some space between us. The song changes, and with my eyes closed, I finally breathe easy again.

Daisy yawns.

"Are you ready to go back to the room?"

She nods at my question. I walk back to the table, my hand not leaving her lower back.

"This was fun, but today was a long day for us, so we're going to bed," I announce, stepping closer to where my parents sit.

"Okay, sweetheart. See you tomorrow, bright and early, to catch the catamaran to Saona."

"Yes, ma'am. Good night everyone."

A mixture of goodnight and buenas noches fills the air. We smile politely, Daisy grabs her purse, and we walk silently to our room. Our room with one bed. As soon as I remember that, I continue the mantra I've been repeating in my head all day, hoping it will become muscle memory at some point and my heart won't get any ideas.

It's just pretend. All of it is just pretend.

We step through the doors, and I finally let go of her hand. Not because I want to, but because there's nobody here, and I promised her I would make her feel comfortable. Holding hands might be too much when this is just pretend.

Daisy swings her hips side to side, stepping forward with long, confident strides, and I have to remind my dick it's just pretend again.

When she turns around and looks at the bed and then at me with concern, I need to remind my heart, the one that skipped a beat at the assumption that she wants me asleep near her, to repeat the mantra over and over again.

But when the concern doesn't leave her eyes, even when time passes, I need to remind my brain I put us in this situation. It's my job to make her feel at ease at the expense of not telling her how I feel…because to her, this is just pretend.

"Hey, it's okay. We're both adults, right?" I chuckle, trying to ease the tension, and she shrugs.

"I snore really loudly," she says, so nonchalantly, it makes me smile.

"Mmmm, you forget who told you that."

A few years ago, we went on a road trip for a weekend after Daisy had been working her ass off for months planning a retirement party for the manager of the Philadelphia Eagles. She was exhausted, so she fell asleep the minute I picked her up. There were no questions about how tired she was and how much she needed the time to just lay down and sleep. She had the softest, cutest snore at the beginning, but as she grew more comfortable and fell into a deeper sleep, it became louder. I was even concerned in moments, thinking she wasn't breathing. She, of course, was fine and just needed rest. When she woke, I called her snoring beauty, and she was appalled, as if she didn't know. Well, I guess she actually didn't know—it was the first time she'd ever been told. She was mortified.

"It's endearing," I say with a smile.

"What if my breath stinks in the morning and I spook you with it?" she asks, bending to remove her sandals. I quickly squat right in front of her, pushing her hands away.

"You could never. Also, my breath might spook *you.*" She's eyeing me skeptically as my fingers graze her ankles, so I add, "Let me."

I remove the strap wrapped around her leg and slide one sandal off, then the other, taking my time without lingering for too long—as much I want to, I don't. I take the pair to the closet, breathing normal and not taking in the completely discombobulated air that's always around Daisy.

"We'll put a pillow barrier for good measure." I change quickly to sweat pants and a t-shirt—not my usual sleeping attire, since I sleep naked. I've never been more glad I packed lounge clothes so I didn't have to have the conversation with Daisy about why I didn't have sleepwear.

"Yeah, yeah. That's fine." She grabs some clothes from her bag and walks to the bathroom, shutting the door behind her. I let a breath out, grab my phone, and lie on the left side of the bed as I wait for Daisy to return. I have maybe five minutes to calm my body and heart and get used to the thought of sharing this bed with her. My words may have been steady, but my body is anything but. I'm charged with energy at the thought of having her so close to me but also filled with dread that I really can't do anything else about it.

The door opens, and with it, my heart jumps. Damn, so much for staying calm. I knew I was doomed from the start, but seeing Daisy in the tiny pajamas she's wearing was not in the cards. At least not in mine. She carries her other clothes to her bag as the micro baseball bat-print shorts hug her legs and her ass in a way that should be illegal. Her arms are free now, revealing a red crop top with baseballs all over it and full breasts with peaked nipples underneath. Damn, what I wouldn't give to lower her top and suck one of them into my mouth. I bet they would fit perfectly in my hands.

Daisy clears her throat, and I snap my eyes to her. "Sorry…I…ummm, the print is very detailed," I mumble. Smooth, Mateo, smooth.

"Oh, this? The team gifted it to me for Christmas last year. A little too small now, but they're my comfort pjs.

Can't get rid of them," she adds, dropping her phone on the nightstand and resting on the bed beside me.

"Not too small. They look great." My attempt in keeping my voice steady fails, and she raises an eyebrow at me.

"Are you okay? You're acting weird. Is this weird? You said it was fine. I—"

"It is fine, I promise," I interrupt. "I'm just tired."

"Okay, then. As long as you're fine, I'm fine." So many fines when I'm anything but fine. My dick is certainly not fine, and neither is my heart.

Mateo, you dumb fuck. You didn't even think to ask if she's comfortable with you here. What a shitty ass friend you are.

"Daze, are you uncomfortable sharing this bed with me?" The panicked look in her eyes makes me think she might be, and I hate myself for it. "I wouldn't do anything you aren't comfortable with. I hope you know that. If this—"

"Oh my God, stop. Yes, yes, I know that. I'm just all in my head about this. You're fine!" She reaches over and turns the lamp off, leaving us in the dark with half her body over my chest.

"Oh! Sorry," she laughs, quickly going to the other side of the bed. The ruffling and pulling at the blanket makes it obvious she's trying to settle herself unsuccessfully. The pressure and sound of her slamming the pillow next to us startles me, and I chuckle. She giggles a little and whispers another sorry.

"Good night!" Her shout echoes through the room, and the bed is finally still.

Her breathing is still labored, but with every ticking second, it eases more and more. I close my eyes and breathe, mirroring her and settling myself.

"Good night, Daisy," I finally whisper, painfully aware of how good she smells, how even her breathing is now, and how warm I feel having her by my side, even if she's not really mine, even if I'm not touching her. Here, on the left side of Daisy's bed, is where I belong. I know it, and I might have to let her know too. I might have to say fuck the rules.

8

He Smells Lick-able
WE CAN'T BE FRIEND BY ARIANA
GRANDE

Daisy

I don't understand what the issue is with Mateo's family and waking up early. Every single time we're making plans to get together or hang out, it's always the same. Be ready by six or else. How can someone live, love, laugh under these conditions? How does anyone live, laugh, love in the 'fake dating your best friend and longest crush at a romantic getaway' condition?

I fell asleep so quickly last night, unlike what I thought would happen. I thought it was going to be absolutely awful, or that I would be perspiring over him sleeping next to me, but instead, my body relaxed. All the way relaxed. Almost as if my brain knew I was safe by his side. I've always felt that, the feeling of belonging next to him, but one bed? That took it to the extreme.

And today, well, fuck me sideways with a double dildo. Today, he's beyond embodying my wildest dreams. Today, he looks edible. He smells lick-able. He feels like mine. *What the hell, Daisy? Edible, lick-able, MINE?*

"What's going on in there today?" Mateo asks, snapping me from the spiral.

"What? Where?" I look around the vast sea, but I don't see anything other than crystal blue waters and a small island in the far distance. Today, we're going to Saona, a government-protected island that, apparently, is like paradise on Earth. We're spending the day there with his family and some of Violeta's family. We've been on this catamaran for about an hour and a half while loud music plays and people drink, dance, and rest. It's beautiful and fun, and I haven't been able to enjoy any of it because I've been spiraling over Mateo.

Mateo chuckles. "In your head, Daze. You've been daydreaming more than usual today. Did you sleep okay?"

Did I sleep okay? Yes, Mateo, I did. Wrapped in the scent of you and your presence, I did.

"I did. I'm just enjoying it all," I reply instead, because I can't tell this man how not only did I sleep great, but when I opened my eyes to the sight of him half naked, his back to me, small droplets of water falling down his back as he shook his hair, I wanted to do very naughty things to him. Wanting my best friend physically, at a molecular level is nothing new, but this level of want? *Fuck.*

"Oye, Mateo. Esa novia tuya se va a quemar si no le pones protector solar en la espalda." He turns around to see whatever it was his cousin said in Spanish while he takes whatever bottle it seems like he's being offered.

"What?" I ask.

"He said you'll get sunburned if I don't put some sunblock on, and he's right. Take this off."

"Take what off?"

"This fishnet thing you have around your body," he

adds, sliding his finger over the edge of my cover up and lifting slightly.

"Excuse me, sir, this is a fashion piece. It's stylish." I remove it swiftly, dropping it on the chair and opening my hand so he can drop the bottle on it.

"Let me," he whispers, swallowing hard, his Adam's apple bobbing, and his eyes holding mine. "Turn around."

I turn, holding in a breath, bracing for when this man lays his hands on me. The minute they come into contact with my skin, it's like the world ceases to exist. The Earth is not spinning anymore. We're not on this boat, and the waves of the ocean are definitely not crashing against it. There's no music. There's nobody else here. Nothing else matters but his hands on my back caressing gently as he applies sunblock starting in the center and slowly spreading out.

Groggy sounds leave his lips. No, not sounds—words. "Relax for me, Daze."

How am I supposed to relax when his hands are on me and he sounds like that? How am I supposed to relax when the act feels so real? I'm so glad this man has not tried to kiss me, because that would do it. That would be the line, I think. The line there's no going back from.

"Alright, lovebirds, let's go!" Livie shouts from somewhere far, snapping the moment in half. Oh, we've made it.

The descriptions and the pictures online did not do this place justice. I thought the sand was white in Romana, where the resort is, but this, this is surreal. The contrast between the almost translucent sand with the turquoise see-through water is breathtaking. The palm trees in the distance with small wooden houses showing artisan products. Oh, markets, they're little markets, not houses. The people welcoming us into the island smile and what seems like merengue plays in the background. So many people playing instruments and dancing in the distance while one by one others from the catamaran get off.

Mateo rushes to the front and offers his hand to every single person who's trying to get off, side by side with Alex. These two mountain-tall men offering smiles and aid to everyone who takes it is endearing... and well, hot.

This is the main issue with my unspoken crush with Mateo. It's not only that he knows me almost better than I know myself—it's that he's also a good human. When most people would do things for show and recognition, he does things like this silently without most people noticing. He's always been like that. Even when he was a hormonal preteen, he always put others first. It sometimes has led him to put himself last, which isn't great for him. Lots of his previous girlfriends had this issue too. It was all about them, them, them, because Mateo, the ultimate book boyfriend he is, would give and give. But relationships are not meant to be like that. Relationships are almost like a dance—effortlessly in sync through the upbeats and the slow tempos. It requires knowing that no matter who's leading, they're in it together. The only way to achieve that is through practice, communication, and trust. But it's also a give and take by way of a connection of harmonies, letting them sink into the body, moving them together.

Most of his past girlfriends were nothing like these. They were more like peg dolls with arms and a little and loud voice screaming, *carry me, no matter how much it takes from you.*

"Daze, you're the last one!" Mateo shouts from the edge, startling me again from my thoughts. If aloof was a person, it would be me on this trip. What the fuck is wrong with me? I grab my bag and offer my hand; instead, he raises his and holds me by the waist, carrying me down effortlessly.

"You're gonna hurt yourself if you keep doing that!"

"You could never hurt me. These—" he taps on his forearms, "were made just to pick you up."

It's when he says shit like this that I get all in my head about the what ifs or the maybes. It's when he says things like this or looks at me the way he is right now that I want to be brave and tell him we can still keep our friendship even if we give us a try. There's something about the way I could love him. I know would be good for him. He deserves to be put first and celebrated beyond what he can do for someone, and I...think I can do that. But then I remember how I'm not his type, so I play it off as him saying something silly, as I always do, because the alternative is too terrifying.

Damn, I'm all in my head about shit again.

We walk in silence toward the beach and his family. The closer we get, the louder the music gets, the more vibrant the place seems, the more I want to just bask in this moment. The fishnet thing, as Mateo called it, is coming off my body, STAT, and I want to just swim, dance, and eat whatever food they're cooking here. I want to try my darndest to either muster the courage to tell Mateo I love him like more than a friend or stop daydreaming about it.

We place our bags onto a chair. Mateo takes his shirt off, and holy shit, the damn body...again. I won't ever get tired of it. It's dizzying and exciting, every time. Every. Single. Time.

"Ready to swim?" he asks with his million dollar smile, and when I nod, he does the one thing I wasn't expecting. Suddenly, his head is by my hip, his arms hugging my thick thighs, and in two seconds flat, I'm upside down and over his shoulder.

"Mateo, what the hell?"

He chuckles. "Let me show you real quick how little I'm worried about you *hurting me*." His voice mimics mine on the last two words as he jogs toward the water without a care in the world.

"Put me down!"

"I will, in the water, head first. No issues with your hair getting wet, right?" He won't stop giggling like a toddler, like this is the funniest thing he has ever done. I've never had an issue with getting my hair wet, especially considering it's so damn straight no matter what I do. What's a little salt water gonna do to it?

The water splashes his legs, and warm droplets hit my face as he runs into the water waist deep and continues deeper. The bouncing of my body and all my rolls jiggling under his hand seem not to faze him in the slightest, and I both want to kiss him and punch him for this.

"Put me—" The words are barely out of my mouth before I'm submerged with strong arms sliding up my ass and landing on my back. We emerge, me breathless and coughing and him smiling while he holds me flushed to him. He brushes the hair off my face before cupping it with his hand. My breathing settles, and I'm completely in a daze of warm, salty water and him.

"Hi," he whispers.

"Hi, right back at you." My voice drops. He holds my gaze, bouncing between my eyes, making me dizzier by the second. His eyes lower to my lips and stay there. Suspended in time. Freezing everything around us once again. I suck in a breath when his pretty brown eyes don't move from my lips. His hand softens the hold he has on my face, going from a protective hold to a more intimate one. Or maybe I'm just imagining the whole thing, and I have a pimple there or something.

I want to say something. *Kiss me.* Do it. Say fuck it. Something! But I can't. Words? What even are those? What's my name? Where are we? None of it. All I can think, breathe, dream of is this man kissing me.

He gets closer, inch by painful inch closer, and right when I think he's going to do it. Right when he's sharing my breath, he turns his face slightly and kisses my cheek instead. Dragging his cheek against mine, he whispers in my ear, "Sorry, they were watching."

I try to turn to see who they are, but he holds me tighter. "Like this. It looks like I'm kissing you. Just put your hands around my neck real quick."

I do as he says, because I clearly have zero self-preservation skills. *Yeah, Daisy, sure. Wrap your hands around his perfect neck while he whispers in your ear and don't fuck this up for everyone involved.*

I'm not breathing, I'm sure of it, but what I am also sure of is his heart beating rapidly under my fingers. I can't move, but what I can do is hear mine thumping so loudly, it's muffling everything around us. So loud, I barely hear Mateo.

"Sorry, if that was too much. Trying not to blow our cover, you know?" he asks, letting go of my face and leaving some space between us.

I clear my throat, gathering any semblance of self-control and dignity I have left. "It's okay. It just took me by surprise is all. I thought you were going to kiss me."

His eyes widen. "Daze, I—"

Splashing behind us alerts me to the end of our privacy as someone gets closer and Mateo stops talking. Good, because I just got confirmation of what I've known my whole life: I'm Mateo's best friend and nothing more…and I will never be anything else.

"I heard we were playing war!" Jaime shouts, dragging

Violeta by the hand. Mateo looks at me, asking for permission, and I nod.

"I do think it's a little unfair. I mean, look how much bigger Daisy is than me," she spits, moving her hand across her body, showing our clear difference in size. Violeta is small. Like maybe extra-small, small. But if she thinks she's going to make me feel bad because I have curves, an ass, and I'm strong? Think again, babe.

"Violeta," Mateo exclaims, letting her know exactly how he feels about her using that tone and those words on me.

I hold his arm, holding him back. I love that he wants to protect me, but I can also fight my own battles. "It's okay. I can play with just one hand if that seems fair to you."

She smiles wickedly at me, and I roll my eyes. "I'll take that as a yes." I turn to face Mateo and whisper to him. "Are you okay with me on your shoulders?"

"I was born to carry you in all ways, Daze. Let's do this!"

There he goes again with his little comments, but I won't let that deter me. This is where Violeta fucked up. There's no one on Earth more competitive than me, and she's about to see a side of me she doesn't know. The volleyball game was child's play, and she was just getting started. She's about to see the side of me that doesn't like to lose. *Let's fucking destroy them!*

Mateo goes under, and in the blink of an eye, my legs are draped around his neck, shoulders dangling in front of him...and I'm up in the air. Half my ass hangs out of this bathing suit, and the warm Caribbean breeze reminds me of it. I quickly reach inside the top of my bathing suit and adjust my boobs. The last thing I need is for one to get out of this and for us to be called out for indecency. Although, maybe not, since I saw plenty of topless women at the beach today and yesterday. Maybe it's common and nobody would care.

Violeta sneers and says, "Let's go."

"Oh no, no. I will call when this starts," Livie says from nearby. I didn't even realize how many of the cousins are here witnessing the show. Well, greeeeat.

Violeta shrugs, and Livie smiles. My girl, always on my side.

"Okay, rules are simple. Bottoms can only push bottoms and tops can only push tops."

"I'll touch a bottom!" one of the cousins shouts from the distance while chaos unravels and Livie rolls her eyes.

"As I was saying, you may not touch the opposite position you're playing." She's so serious, as if this is a real game with high stakes.

"This isn't football, shortie," Alex says, and we all laugh.

"This is serious though. So hush and listen. I heard Daisy say she'll only play with one hand. Are you serious?" she asks.

"Sure. Keeping it fair, since she seems to have a problem with me being thick and bigger than her."

Ohs, oohs, and claps surround us, and I smile at Violeta. She rolls her eyes this time and glares at me. Two can play this game, especially considering there's absolutely no reason for this girl to be mean to me right now.

"Don't pull each other's bathing suits down. Don't pull each other's hair. Don't pinch, and definitely no spitting. Keep your feet to yourself too—no kicking."

"They're not toddlers," Tere says, and Livie narrows her eyes. She raises her hands in defeat. "Fine, your rules."

"I'm keeping it fair. Am I clear?" Livie asks, and we nod. "First couple to go under loses, and the one left standing will be the champion of round one. We can keep playing if you want. Ready?"

"Ready!" Mateo and I shout.

Violeta and Jaime say, "Sí."

"Dale!" Livie shouts, and Jaime and Mateo go at it. I keep my left hand behind my back and let Violeta come to me. She's acting erratic, so staying calm will be my strength today.

Her hands fly to my shoulders, and she pushes. Or at least she tries to. She was right about one thing: I don't think it's fair. Not because I'm bigger than her, but because I'm stronger. If I remember correctly, Violeta hates lifting weights because she's afraid it will make her look masculine or whatever that means. She's too worried about looking and acting like Barbie that she can't see the biggest disadvantage she has is that I'm athletic and strong. Always have been, always will be.

I lock my hand on her shoulder, shoving her back slightly. I don't apply too much pressure because I don't want to hurt her, but she still flinches. Jaime and Mateo are going at it, but they're both holding strong. I push Violeta a little harder, and she wobbles. She narrows her eyes and lets out a cry that could be a grunt or curse. Either way, I don't let it deter me from the task at hand. I lean forward, holding on to Mateo with my feet under his arms. With one last push, she's going backwards, and Mateo uses the momentum to also push his cousin down, both of them falling into the water.

"Woohoo!" I shout, lifting my arms in the air as Mateo spins us around. I lower my hands immediately and hold his head with a yelp. "Stop it!"

He chuckles and lowers me to the water. I slide off, and once we're both back at the same level, he holds me in his arms and whispers, "I knew you could do it."

I wink and turn to the group, who are all clapping. Except Violeta, obviously.

"Good game," I say, extending my hand, which she takes but doesn't say anything else.

I look at Mateo, and as soon as he's done shaking Jaime's hand, he's back by my side, smiling like a little kid on his birthday. This is what makes it harder, knowing that he's not only my favorite person and best friend, but also how much fun we have together. I can't risk losing that by telling him how I feel and making things awkward. I shake my head and my feelings away, just like I always do, and smile at everyone.

"Who's next?" I ask.

9

How Fond Are You of This Underwear?

SI SUPIERAS BY DADDY YANKEE & WISIN & YANDEL - BACHATA ROSA BY JUAN LUIS GUERRA & PERFECT TIMING BY HURTS

Mateo

"Daisy, we have to go," I call from the other side of the bathroom door.

We slept in this morning, or at least she did. I couldn't sleep past six, especially considering she was making the cutest sounds all night. I woke up with my face practically nuzzled in her neck. It startled me, so I got up and went for a run. Running so I don't tell her exactly how I feel. Running so I don't fuck things up or scare her.

But not even that could erase her telling me she thought I was going to kiss her. Was she disgusted at the thought, or was she excited at the possibility? Was she looking forward to it? For the first time in forever, I couldn't read her. It seemed for a second like she wanted to, but maybe it was *my* want translating into what I thought was hers. We're minutes away from being late to the rehearsal dinner, but she won't come out.

"I know. I just don't think I can go." The door opens

revealing a stunning and absolutely breathtaking Daisy. She's wearing a teal and turquoise dress, her hair bouncing in soft waves above her shoulders. The dress molds to her body perfectly, enhancing all her curves, and the giant slit on the side shows her leg almost all the way to her hip. I swallow hard and dare to meet her eyes. Her eyebrows are lifted, her head tilted to the side…and I've been busted.

"You look incredible, Daze," I whisper, holding her gaze.

"This dress is a lot smaller than I thought. I'm usually good about trying shit on before I wear it, but I didn't have time before the trip. When I bought it, it fit just fine, but now I look like I'm wrapped up bubble gum."

"What?" I chuckle.

"Look! It's like a teal wrapper, and I'm just a piece of chunky gum. I can't go like this." Her hands roam her body, as if I needed a reminder of how she looks. My dick definitely doesn't need the reminder, that's for sure. This is better than what she looks like in my dreams. The reality of Daisy is more than my mind can conjure in any wishing spell.

"You look not only stunning, but hot. Your dress is perfect, and the color suits you. If you're uncomfortable, then don't wear it, but…I think it looks amazing."

She blushes and tosses a piece of her hair over to the side. "I'm not uncomfortable… but don't I look ridiculous?"

"Ridiculously beautiful, if I dare say so." She looks at me with skepticism in her eyes. "I mean it. That dress was made for you," I echo, hoping to leave no doubt in her mind I'm for real.

"Okaaaay, let's go then. We're already late." She passes by, flowers and something sweet hugging me as she walks toward the door.

I'm never going to be immune to the way she smells. The way she talks. The way she walks, laughs, sleeps. The way she simply exists. We walk in silence to the restaurant. She's probably concerned about the millions of things she's always concerned about, and I'm trying to muster the courage to tell her how much she means to me.

After the whole war fiasco yesterday, Violeta realized there was nothing she could do to piss me or Daisy off, and she let us be. We actually got to enjoy Saona. We spent most of the day with my family, but today was just for us to hang out and relax. I wasn't able to relax much, though, because Daisy has been pretty much giving me the cold shoulder all day. She's talked to me but about nothing particular, just whatever I ask. We're all going to be together for the rehearsal dinner, so the aunts and uncles didn't want to push for more activities.

Daisy was working at some point, even though I refused. I need to rest, and this is the only way I'll be able to reset and be ready to get back to work after Christmas. She thought I was working the day before, but I was really just keeping myself entertained so as not to think about her naked in the shower just steps away.

Dinner passes without a hiccup, and although Daisy easily pretends she's mine, she's not okay. I can feel it in my bones. Now, we're all in the resort's club, drinking, dancing, and talking. Daisy has been glued to my side but talking to Livie most of the night. She hasn't looked my way much, even though she lets me wrap my arms around her or even kiss her head. I don't know what happened, and I wish she would just give me a sign.

I can't take my eyes off her no matter how much I try. Not now, when she's dancing with one of my cousins. Not when people talk to me. Not ever. Even if she's upset at me for some reason.

"You know…people who are fake dating their best friends don't look at them like that."

"Like what?" I ask my sister, who's grinning from ear to ear.

"Like you'd want to marry her one day. Alex looks at me like that, you know? Why don't you just tell her?"

"Tell her what?" I know she's smart, and maybe playing coy is an insult to her intelligence, but I can't flat out say it. Not without telling Daisy first.

"That you love her."

"I've told her I love her our whole lives."

"Not like that, big bro. When are you going to push for more? When are you going to take the shot? You're usually a go-getter. An overachiever. A dream bigger and shoot higher kind of guy. I've always admired that about you." She pauses to look at Daisy. "I've always wondered why you play it safe with Daisy." Livie's not wrong. I take risks, I try hard things, I never give up, I never quit, so why can't I with her? Why can't I be brave around Daisy?

Then, it hits me. I can't be brave, not when…"I'm afraid."

Livie nods and smiles softly at me. "Fear, we can work with. So tell me: what's the worst that can happen?"

I open my mouth to answer but stop myself to ponder her question. What would be the worst-case scenario? She doesn't feel the same, and I'm left brokenhearted? She thinks I'm joking and plays it off as she usually does when I try to hint at something more? What is it? I look back at the two decades of friendship we share, and the answer is as clear as day.

"That she won't be my friend anymore."

Livie smiles and nods looking at the dance floor. I follow her gaze and find a very rosy-cheeked and very happy Daisy trying her best to keep up with my dad's dance moves. I love that my family loves her this much—almost as much as I do.

"Do you really think anything can ruin your friendship?" Livie asks.

Honestly…probably not. Nothing has through over two decades. Not different schools or going to college. Not relationships or time and space. I'm meant to be hers, in any capacity. I shake my head in answer, and she nods.

"Then just be honest with her. Is friendship really a friendship if you're hiding something that big from her?"

"I guess not."

"Then man up and tell her. Also…you're like a bazillion years old. Grow up a little, big bro." She pats my back, hops out of her seat, and bounces on the balls on her feet all the way to Alex's lap. He welcomes her with a smile; it warms my heart that my little sister found someone who loves her the way she deserves to be loved.

"¿Puedo?" I ask my father as soon as I join them on the dance floor.

"Claro, muchacho. ¡Esta niña me va a sacar el jugo! ¡Dale, dale!" I laugh at his words as he walks back to the table.

"What did he say?" Daisy asks.

"That you're gonna run him dry."

We both laugh. I hold Daisy's hand and bring her to me, slowing us down to match the bachata playing. It's almost like fate; the DJ must know how much I love dancing bachata—how much I love dancing with her. Daisy always being around in my house meant she was there for the early Saturday mornings when Aventura, Juan Luis Guerra, Gilberto Santa Rosa, or Anthony Santos were playing. It meant my dad was walking around dancing with anything that moved, teaching us the steps. My mother silently drank her café con leche and read the newspaper while us kids learned side steps and how to follow rhythm. Daisy is no stranger to any of my favorite Dominican and Puerto Rican singers, and I love that about her.

"I love your family," she whispers. *I love you*, I want to say, but I keep it inside. We fall into a silent dance beyond what our mouths say. This silence is deeper. She won't talk. She won't look at me. The only communication between us is the coordination of our bodies and how she melts in my hands. Even if she's upset at me, her body talks. Her body is comfortable with me. Her body feels safe with me.

"What's going on, Daze?" I ask, keeping my voice soft.

"Nothing," she mumbles without turning to look at. Yeah, nothing my ass.

"Talk to me. What's going on?"

"Nothing," she echoes.

"Then why won't you look at me?"

She finally does. She snaps her eyes to mine, and I find fear there.

"Daisy, what's going on? Did someone hurt you?" I bring my hand to hold her face. Her skin is warm under my palm, and she closes her eyes as she stops dancing. The music keeps going, but it feels far away. We're both standing here, caught in this strange moment of stillness, looking at each other while the room spins around us.

"Stop looking at me like that." Her words are sharp, and I flinch at the sudden coldness in her voice.

"Like what?" My chest tightens. I'm usually a very smart person, quick to see patterns, quick to read people, quick to read her, but I can't figure this one out at all.

"Like I'm delicate and precious, and you might die if something happens to me." Her eyes dart away.

"Well, then I can't, because all of those things are true.

Don't you know how much you mean to me?" My voice cracks.

"I do. I know you love me and I'm your best friend. I do. I know I'm important to you. I'm just…all in my head, I guess." She bites her lip, shoulders folding in. She's retreating again, and it's killing me that I don't know what's going on.

"All in your head about what?" She may not speak but her eyes are loud and clear in this moment. "Just say it Daisy. All in your head about what?"

"I thought you were gonna kiss me yesterday, okay? I thought you *wanted* to kiss me. And I was giddy and it was dumb and clearly, you don't feel that way about me and it's fine and just know I love you and our friendship and maybe I just didn't think about this whole thing long enough because—" She stops herself with her eyes wide open. "Oh shit. Never mind. Just ignore me."

I shake my head, smiling at her. Holy hell, Daisy might actually feel the same way. I hold her hand and lead us out of the room straight to the pool area, and even though it's night, I look around to make sure we're alone. We're not—there's a couple in the water, acting very, *very* cozy, so this is not the right spot. I lead us fast and steady past the pool bar, past the giant wall and the flowers.

"Where are we going?" The night sky shines bright above us, but I don't reply. I keep leading us down the stone walkway and onto the sand. I slow our steps since Daisy is wearing heels. The last thing I need is for her to break an ankle.

It's dark, the stars shining bright above us, the path lit with lights hidden in the ground and around the bushes, but it's still quiet and calm. The crashing of the waves against the shore are the only sounds I need for this moment. I turn around and walk Daisy back against a coconut tree and close the space between us.

"Ask me why I didn't kiss you," I whisper, my voice laced with desire.

"What?"

"Ask. Me. Why. I. Didn't. Kiss. You." I accentuate every word, closing the inches between us. We're so close, I can almost taste her. So close, all I breathe is her. All I see is her.

"Why didn't you kiss me?" she finally asks. Her voice is soft, almost shy, as if she truly doesn't want to know and she's just asking me because I prompted her.

"Because when I finally do kiss you, I don't want there to be a doubt in your mind. When I finally taste you for the first time, I want you to know exactly why."

She catches a breath when my eyes trail to her lips. I don't expect her to say anything, but she does, forever the beautiful chatter box she is.

"I would know what, exactly?" she asks, and I smile at her, placing one hand by her head, caging her in.

"How much I've wanted to kiss you practically my whole life." She gasps, but I don't wait a second longer. I hold her face and lower mine down to meet hers. The minute my lips touch hers, I know there's no going back. There is no way in hell I can let Daisy go. It was never going to happen, but now, even more so. Whatever it takes, whatever convincing she might need, she's mine, and I'm about to show her.

I kiss her softly at first, slowly, exploring those lips I've memorized all my life. I lick every crease, the edge where they touch as she opens for me. I explore her mouth, the inside of her lips and her tongue, like if I don't commit to memory every space, I might die. Her tongue is matching every stroke of mine, completely driving me wild. Her hands climb up my back delicately, pulling gently at my hair at the nape. She moans, and I groan when I deepen the kiss.

I kiss her for who knows how long, because again, everything is frozen but her. Nothing exists; *I* barely exist with her lips on mine. Death by Daisy's kiss could be on my tombstone; if this is how I go, I'd be a happy man. Somehow, the space between us is too much, and she feels it too, because she opens her mouth wider, pulling my hair tighter between moans and cries that die on my lips. *Damn, she's so hot.*

I hold her hip and close the small space between us. My dick presses against her, and she widens her stance, allowing me in. *Damn, so hot.*

We kiss, lick, bite. We moan and gasp and grab. Desperate for each other. Desperate for more. Her hands are frantically exploring while mine hold us steady. I push my pelvis forward, and as she opens her legs wider, I thank my lucky stars for the slit in her dress that immediately allows access to her core. I push up as she draws a circle around my dick, and we both moan. I let go of her lips and look at her, asking for permission or mercy, I'm not sure which. It's definitely one or the other, because I can't hold it in anymore. I'm willing to be patient and go slow if she needs me to, but then, I need a breather. I need to walk. I need a shower.

Daisy doesn't say anything. She just looks at me, panting, while my dick is nestled against her sex, while her thighs house mine. Maybe this is too much for her. Maybe this is too fast.

"We don't have to do anything, Daisy. We can take this slow if you want. I'd wait a million years for you."

"Fuck slow. I've been waiting my whole damn life. I'm

yours to do with as you wish, Teo. I'm here. Just make me feel good."

I crash my lips to hers again, but this time, there's no doubt or hesitation. I might have to fuck her right on this beach if that's what it takes, but someone's going to cum, and it's not going to be me first. We kiss and lick again, and she opens her mouth wider as she grinds on my hardness.

"You're so fucking hot, baby," I pant against her lips, and she moans again.

"Call me baby again," she pleads as she twirls her hips once more.

I pinch her nipple over her dress, and she repeats the movement, tighter this time as she drops her head back. *That's it.* "Are you gonna keep grinding that tight little cunt right on me, baby?"

"Oh." Her word comes out soft, and she does exactly that.

"May I?" I ask, bringing my fingers to the thin strap of her dress. She looks around before she replies. "We're alone, I promise," I continue as she nods. I lower her strap, pulling it down her arm and helping her out of it. The top of her dress is tight around her breasts, so it requires more than just slipping it off her shoulder. I don't care—I'll take whatever steps necessary to give her the pleasure she deserves.

I pull the fabric carefully, successfully lowering it enough for me to see her bare, full breasts, round and perfect in front of me.

"Sorry, they're not cute and perky," Daisy whispers.

"Don't apologize for having these. They're perfect. Look," I say, bringing my hand to cup one.

"It fits perfectly in my hand." *Just like I dreamed it did. Fuck, but better.*

I lower my mouth to the other one, bringing her

peaked nipple to my mouth and sucking it gently in. She hisses.

"You fit perfectly in my mouth too," I say with a mouthful of the most perfect tit a man has ever seen and tasted. I lick and bite around her nipple while my hand pinches the other one, escalating this moment into more. She arches her back against the trunk of the tree, pushing her breast further into my mouth. Fuck, she likes it, almost as much as I do. She's driving me wild, with her hips bucking and her breast filling my mouth. My hand is full of her, and still, I need more.

I explore. My hand curves down to her hip, and as if she can tell exactly what I'm thinking, she moves the fabric over her leg. Thank you to whoever designed this dress, because this slit is perfect for exactly what I want to do to her right now.

My fingers find the edge of her panties and follow the hem to the sensitive area I've been dying to touch. She parts her legs for me before tensing.

"It's not you," she whispers, and I stop. I find her looking at me with concern. "I…I'm not super wet, I know it, but it's not you, it's—"

"Your PCOS, I know," I say. I stand straight, keeping my fingers under the hem of her underwear while my other hand comes up to hold her face.

"You know? How?"

"When you got diagnosed and you told me, I spent weeks reading about it. It was one of the things that lots of articles mentioned: low lubrication and difficulty reaching orgasms."

"Why did you read about it?" Her face looks puzzled, as if it's a big deal, like she can't imagine someone who cares about her reading about a condition that affects her every day.

"Because it's a part of you. Why else do you think every month I bring you ice packs, warm compresses, and massage your back with CBD oil? We also watch all those movies you like."

"Mmm, because I'm usually on my period. I've always wondered how you know."

"I track it so I can help you feel better." It's true. I've read so much about how symptoms can be stronger for women with PCOS, so I try my best to help when I can.

"What if my period isn't regular, like most people with this?" she asks, and I guess we're having this whole ass conversation right now. Out of all the times in the world, she chooses to have it now, when I just want to touch and kiss her and make her feel good. Peace of mind over anything, I guess.

"I would figure it out, Daze. I've made it my mission to learn everything about you, including your body." I kiss her collarbone and then her cheek. "Getting to know what you like, what bothers you, what makes you feel good, what makes you feel better, has always been a priority of mine. If I had to delete my app and figure it out based on subtle cues, I would." I kiss her again, letting the words rest in her mind. Maybe she'll finally see how gone for her I am.

"And you enjoy that?" she asks shyly.

"I love making you my priority, Daisy girl, one chick flick and warm compress at a time." My smile against her skin widens, breathing her in.

"I'm not worried about you not being wet or whatever. I will make you feel good, I promise." I kiss her lips as a small tear leaves her eye. "I've got you, baby, always. Now, can I continue?"

She chuckles and nods, bringing my lips to hers and kissing breathlessly. I take advantage of her lips on mine to bring my hand up and away from her pelvis.

"Wait…" She always begs, and I smile. I love her.

"I'm not done. I just need you to do something for me," I say.

"Anything."

I put two fingers to her lips and whisper, "Suck, baby. Make them sloppy wet for me." Her eyes widen, but she does as I say. Who would've thought that little miss *I can do it all* likes to be bossed around a little bit. Once my fingers are wet, I bring them back to the edge of her panties and slowly drag them between her folds, finding her hard clit and quivering at the touch. The thrill of knowing how responsive she is to my touch is the most perfect surprise. I knew deep down we were meant for each other, but damn.

"Jesus," she whispers when I circle her clit twice.

"Oh, don't bring him into this. Just you and me here, baby. Nobody else."

I circle her clit a few more times until her head hits the trunk and she lets out those breathy sounds again. I kiss her neck, behind her ear, right on her collarbone. I press against her clit when I suck on her skin, and she whispers sounds that go straight to my dick.

"More," she says loud and clear. *I hear you, baby, I hear you.*

"How fond are you of these underwear?" I ask against her ear.

"They're cheap, so not very. Why?" The words are barely out of her mouth when I rip the panties off her in one quick tug.

She gasps. "Teo!"

"You said they were cheap. I'd buy you a dozen more, even if they weren't just to be able to do this." I grab between her legs and hold it tightly. "Fits perfectly too."

"I can buy my own underwear, thank you very much."

I cock my head to the side, and the way she smiles makes me tremble.

"What are you going to do about it now, though?" she asks. So damn naughty. So perfectly naughty.

I kiss her feisty mouth and press over her clit. Gently at first, but as she rocks, I apply pressure. She bites my lower lip, and I see stars, but not the ones in the sky. No, I see *her.* I groan when I feel her clit tighten more.

"Teo," she whispers against my lips.

"You're so hot when you say my name like that, all breathy and needy. Do you want me to fuck you with my fingers, baby?"

She nods and closes her eyes.

"Use your words, Daze."

"Yes, please."

"So polite. So perfect. So mine." I slide my finger in, exploring, seeing how much she can take before she unravels. Her pussy tightens around my finger immediately, her walls closing in as my dick jerks in response.

I slide the finger out, and she whimpers an impatient sigh.

"Patience is a virtue, baby." I bring my finger to my mouth and taste her arousal. I just know I'll be craving this forever. "You taste addicting."

I spit on my fingers, and she widens her eyes, tracking my movements. As soon as my fingers are back at her entrance, she tenses. I lower my lips to her ear and whisper, "Relax for me, Daze."

As if on cue, she does, relaxing her legs and letting out a breath, allowing my fingers entrance, welcoming them with a gasp.

I hold her neck with one hand and bite her earlobe as my fingers pump in and out of her. "I can't get enough of you against my body. Of the feel of you everywhere."

"Please," she whispers.

"Please what, baby?"

"I need more. Please." She lets out a sigh. I pick up the tempo, my thumb landing on her clit while my fingers keep pumping in and out.

"I have what you need. Just let yourself feel it." I sink my fingers deeper, arching them, finding the spot I was looking for.

"That feels so good," she echoes, and I continue my movements. My hand leaves her neck to hold her hip in place instead. She likes my fingers digging into her skin, because as soon as I do, she opens wider. Bingo.

"That's it, baby. Chase it." She swirls her hips, and if it takes her two hours to get it, with my fingers caressing that spot she seems to enjoy, so be it. Who needs a hand?

"Do you want me to lick your pussy, Daze?"

"Oh," she whispers.

"Words," I command.

"Yes," she breathes.

I kiss her neck again, moving down her body, kissing her nipple and making her hiss. *Tender, got it.* I kneel in front of her, dragging my hand away from her hip, up her thighs to grab her ass. I dig in with my fingertips at the same time my tongue splits her folds and licks her clit.

"Teo!" she shouts in what sounds like both a groan and a whisper, and it makes me groan against her sex. She squeezes tight around my fingers.

"You like that, huh?"

"Yes."

I lick and tease her clit, pumping my fingers in and out of her relentlessly. I spit again, this time letting it roll down her clit to her entrance. I take advantage of it and slide another finger in.

"Damn," she says on a gasp.

"You wanted more. Let me give you what you need." I let her adjust to the invasion of my fingers while I lick her senseless. She bucks her hips against me, her hand slipping into my hair and tugging slightly, tilting my head back. I open my eyes and find her looking down at me.

"You're a vision," I whisper before returning to my mission: making Daisy come undone under my tongue. I keep teasing, kissing, licking, not removing my eyes from her and not stopping my fingers from pumping.

"You're gonna make me come," she says, and I hum.

"That's it, give it to me." I bite her clit, sucking it into my mouth.

"Mateo!" she shouts as she becomes a writhing mess in front of me.

Her nails dig into my neck and her legs close, almost wrapping around my face. If this is how I die—suffocated by this woman—I'll die a happy man. I slow my tongue as her breathing evens out and her legs stop shaking. I get up, picking up the discarded panties and tucking them in my pocket. There shouldn't be any littering at any beach, ever.

Daisy's eyes are still closed, her lips parted slightly, her breath coming in short bursts, and it pulls a smile from my lips at the sight. I smooth her dress down her legs and kiss her dampened cheek.

"As much as I loved the exhilaration of this moment, I would like nothing more than to continue it in our bedroom."

Her eyes snap open the minute the word *our* leaves my lips.

"There is only one bed, after all," I say with a wink, and she giggles. Okay, good. She breathes out, relaxing, just how I like it.

I take her hand and guide us back to our hotel room, quietly enjoying the salty breeze on our faces and trying to commit what just happened to memory.

10

Swallow

GLOW BY KELLY CLARKSON FT. CHRIS STAPLETON & RELACIÓN BY SECH, DADDY YANKEE & J BALVIN FT. ROSALIA & FARRUKO

Daisy

I died and went to heaven. A heaven with Mateo's tongue between my legs. A tongue that worked hard to make me come. A tongue that said he knew I don't lubricate well because he studied PCOS? Who the fuck does that? I knew he was a good friend, but damn.

"Can I ask you something?" I ask as soon as he opens the door and we step through.

"Is the question can we do that again? Because the answer is yes, right now."

Heat rises in my cheeks at his words and the mischief behind his eyes. So smooth. So, so smooth.

"You said you knew about the, mm, um—"

"Lubrication?" he interrupts, and I nod. "Don't get shy on me now, Daze. We're still us, just with an added layer. A layer I've been dying to add for years."

I'm at a loss for words. *Years*? What does he mean,

years? What? No, no. Focus, Daisy, focus. "We're gonna talk about what that means later. My question was…why? Why did you read about it?"

He holds my hands and softens his features, smiling at me. "Because it's a part of who you are. Why do you think I always order the broccoli salad?"

I give him a once-over and furrow my brows. "I thought you liked it?"

"Broccoli helps with hormone balancing. I asked Ms. Kim about the ingredients and asked if she could start adding apple cider vinegar, which also helps. She thinks it's for me because I didn't want to talk about your business with everyone, but yeah, that's why."

I'm dumbfounded. "That is the sweetest thing anyone has ever done for me."

"It's not that hard. I care about you, Daze. All of you. If I can do anything to help, I'm going to do it." His hand comes to my cheek with a half-smile painted on his face.

"Well, nobody has ever done that or anything like it. I…" I pause to think about whether I want to say this. Do I want to be this vulnerable with him while his beard is still coated with me? But this is Mateo. *My Mateo.* My best friend. My everything. And he…what? Also wants me?

"Just say it. Whatever it is. I'm here."

Alright, Daisy, big girl pants on. Boss babe attitude. Just tell him. "I actually have never had someone understand how I'm not all wet and shit, the way movies and books describe women when they're aroused. I usually carry lube with me everywhere I go. And for you…it was just so…I don't know."

"Normal? Compassionate? Hot?"

"Teo," I whisper. " I don't think you understand."

"No, I don't think *you* understand, Daisy girl. Do you

know for how long I've dreamed of kissing you? Of touching you? Of hearing you whisper my name like that? All breathy and spent?" The intensity behind his gaze is making me quiver where I stand.

He continues. "Years. Not days, not months, years. It never felt like the right place or the right time. It's still scary as shit, because our friendship is the most valuable thing to me. I would never do anything to jeopardize it." He holds my face again, and I lean in to his touch.

"But baby, making you feel good, helping you feel good, has been a priority all my life. I'm just glad I could show you other ways I can make that happen."

I gasp.

"All I want to know is if you feel the same way." Not only is this man bringing everything out in the open, leaving no doubt in my mind about his feelings, but he's also terrified that they might not be reciprocated. I can see it—the fear behind his eyes. I try to open my mouth to tell him, but he raises his hand. "Because if you don't and you just got carried away on this trip, that's fine too. I will continue fantasizing about you instead, but I need to keep you. Your friendship is mine, and I won't risk it. So whatever I—"

I crash my lips to his, tasting mint and something tangy I'm assuming is me. I explore his lips the way he explored mine earlier and letting him know without words exactly how I feel. Did I wish upon a star or something? Because this, right here, are dreams coming true. He backs me against the wall, pinning me in place with his body, just like earlier. And I see stars. This time behind my eyes and not in the nighttime sky.

He's hard against me again, or maybe still. I didn't take care of him. I cup his hard dick in my hand, and he moans against my lips.

Well, fuck me sideways. That's hot.

"I want this so bad, but I'm all sandy, sweaty, and gross," I whisper against his lips.

"We can fix that. Lift your arms for me," he says. I do, no questions asked, but it's not until he lowers the zipper that I realize what's happening.

"Paid attention to where that zipper was much?" I mention between giggles.

He drags my dress off my shoulders and helps me step out. His eyes flare when he sees my body completely exposed, considering he ripped my panties off. That just became a core memory, one I will never forget.

"I memorize everything about you. I always need material for my dreams. I wish I knew how to draw so I can repeat each image and keep you forever, but my memory will have to suffice in the meantime."

"The fuck? You've always had this smooth-ass talk hiding behind the cordial talk and the pretty, beard-covered smiles?"

"I've been saying all my truths for years. You just brushed them off as me joking around."

I hold his gaze, searching for a lie I won't find. I replay a thousand little moments when she showed me the truth, and I just ignored it. I know deep down that he's always been mine. I just needed to listen. He rakes his pretty brown eyes all over my body, igniting every inch of my skin without a single touch while he stands there all smug and looking fantastic with his light blue suit and his white shirt barely buttoned up.

"You know it really isn't fair that I have no clothes on and you have all that."

"Do you want to see me naked, Daisy girl?"

"Please," I plead, and he smiles wickedly.

He steps out of his shoes, unbuckles his belt, and slowly

takes his pants off. He won't stop looking at me, and I can't stop staring either. His strong legs look perfect with the tight black briefs he's wearing, and once his shirt and jacket are on the ground, I get to marvel at his perfect torso. Mateo is an athlete, always has been, and his body is here to remind me of that. So hard. So solid. All straight lines and absolutely mouthwatering. His hair is still tightly styled backwards, but I like his hair free and messy, so I lift my hands up and shake it loose. His soft curls bounce almost immediately out of the gel, but they're still not as soft as I like. Water can fix that, though.

"I love your hair," I whisper with a smile on my face.

"I love yours too. This haircut killed me when I saw it."

I shake my head. "This?"

He groans and rakes his fingers through my hair, whispering against my lips, "Yes." He kisses me tenderly, his hands intertwined in my hair and mine pulling him slightly.

I clear my throat. "You still have clothes on."

His hooded eyes darken, and instead of chestnut brown, they're more like mahogany now. Oh shit.

"If you want to see my dick so badly, why don't you take it out?" This man's mouth. So filthy, I would have never imagined.

"Gladly," I bite back, dragging my hands down his hard body and holding his briefs at the edge. I lower them, painfully slow, until his massive dick springs free. Once his briefs are on the floor and he steps out of them, I can't stop gaping. His dick is not only big, but it's thick too. Well fuckety fuck. A challenge, alright. The veins around it are detailed enough that they look like trails, and the head is the perfect shape to lick. Damn, my mouth is watering now.

Mateo chuckles. I look up and raise an eyebrow.

"It won't bite," he jokes.

"Ha ha, so funny. It might choke me to death, though." He chuckles. "That might kill me, Teo."

His laugh bounces off the walls and fills my heart. Good; find the joy in this embarrassing situation.

"You do not have to suck my dick, Daisy. Come on, let's shower," he says.

I raise an eyebrow and cock my head. "You don't think I can?" Maybe it's the competitiveness in me or the fact that I'm practically salivating at the idea, but something sparks within me, and I drop to my knees in front of him.

"I think you can do anything you want, but I don't want you to do it just to prove a point."

"Watch me suck it like a pro," I say, mustering courage I didn't know I had.

"Daisy," he mumbles the minute my hands grab his ass.

"Mm-hmm?"

"You—"

I swirl my tongue around his tip.

"Fuck," he groans.

"You were saying?" I lick from the base all the way to the tip.

He closes his eyes and groans again.

"Watch me, Teo," I command, and his eyes, fringed with long lashes and want, snap open to meet mine. I hold his dick with one hand while I pull him closer by his perfectly round ass. I start slowly relaxing my mouth around him, letting him go deeper and deeper. I don't take my eyes off him, so I'm sure he sees the panic before I say anything at all, and he pulls back away from me.

"Let's take a shower. It's fine," he says.

I narrow my eyes on him. "Do you not want me like this? On my knees, ready to gag on your dick?"

He groans again.

"I can be such a good girl. Wanna see?" I tease again.

"Jesus, Daze."

"Oh, what was it that you said earlier? Don't bring him into this, he's not here. I'm your god now." I smirk, licking my lips when his dick twitches.

"Are you sure you're real?" he asks. "You're so damn perfect."

"Thank you, I know. Now, if you'll excuse me, I would love to taste you again." I swirl around his tip again and blow gently on it. He tenses, and I follow it by bringing his dick into my mouth again. Slowly, I make my way up and down his shaft, flattening my tongue and welcoming the stretch. It's so powerful knowing this man, as hot as he is, standing in front of me, feels so much pleasure at the expense of my tongue.

I moan around it when I taste a little bit of salt on the back of my throat.

"Daze," he groans.

"Mm," I hum, relaxing my mouth and throat and taking him deeper.

He brings his hand to my head, and I hum in agreement. Yes, please. Make me choke on it. As if he can read my mind, he pushes his hips slightly forward, and I groan, not taking my eyes off him.

"You'll be my undoing."

He wraps my hair around his fist and pulls gently, making me moan again. I spread my thighs and lower my hand between my legs. I need friction. I need pressure. I need something.

I bob my head back and forth, flattening my tongue as much as it can while making sloppy, indecent sounds at the taste of him. He doesn't take his eyes off me, just how I want it, as he pushes gently forward, holding my head in place and pulling my hair.

I apply more pressure, closing my lips tighter around his dick while I stroke my clit with two fingers. This is the hottest thing I've ever experienced, and he seems to think the same, gauging by the way he's looking at me.

I suck, taking him deeper, groaning when he tenses.

"If you don't want my cum down your throat, you need to stop now." I hum in response. I don't know how he's even able to form coherent thoughts, but I speed it up, taking him deeper, moaning against him. *Give it to me*, I ask silently. I touch myself harder.

He holds my head tighter, shoving his dick deeper and making tears stream down my face. His eyes open wide, and he tries to pull back at the sight. I shake my head. I'm not done, and he doesn't get to tell me what I can or cannot handle. I take him deeper, gagging around him, but I relax, breathing through my nose one last time before taking his dick all the way to my throat.

"Daze," he shouts and pushes his dick deeper again, shooting warm and salty cum down my throat. I take it all in my mouth, slowing the pace and breathing through my nose, but I don't swallow. I want all of it in my mouth before I do. I want a mouth full of his release, knowing I did this to him. He pulls out of my mouth, painfully slow, drawing the moment out. I'm unwell. Unwell and I loved it.

"Did you swallow?" I shake my head, my mouth full of his cum, a closed lip smile plastered on my face.

His eyes flare again. "Show me."

I open my mouth wide and show him every bit of cum I'm holding like the damn good girl I told him I could be.

"Before you swallow…" I cock an eyebrow, careful not to spill any. "…spit some in your hand." Well, fuck. I nod and do as he says, no questions asked, making a mess everywhere.

"Look at me," he demands again. I *love* bossy Mateo. "Swallow." I do as he says. We didn't even make it to the bathroom, so here I am, on my knees, cum running down my throat while I hold some in my hand and my clit pulses for this man.

"So obedient."

"Yes, sir," I tease, making him groan again.

His cum is starting to drip down my hand, but he doesn't mention it. He just guides me slightly onto the ground so my back is laying on the cold floor, and I hiss.

"I know how you like your bed clean, so let's just make a mess of the floor, yeah?" He knows me so well.

"Spread my cum all over your pretty pussy." His orders are doing more to me than any touch could. I don't question him; I just follow his command. My legs are partially closed, and he shakes his head.

"Open up and let me watch." He's still standing over me while I lie at his feet, completely exposed.

This is so fucking hot, and I don't even know why. I'm so turned on, it won't take long to make me come again, even if I just touch myself. A record for sure. I drag my fingers between my folds, spreading his cum, and when I don't have anymore, I slide two fingers in. If I don't get filled by something quickly, I might actually die.

"Atta girl."

Well, fuck.

I moan, my fingers sliding in and out as I arch my back, not taking my eyes off Mateo. Mateo, who is lowering to his knees in front of me. Mateo, who moves my fingers out of my pussy. Mateo, who lays his head between my legs, his hands holding my thighs in place. He licks his cum off me, and God, there's no way this is real. There's just no way.

"Mmm, something about you and me mixed together is euphoric," he says.

"You can't say shit like that and expect me to be fine after this," I whisper.

"Am I ruining you, Daisy girl?" He lifts his face, looking at me from between my legs. I'm resting on my elbows, looking at this man who devoured me earlier, and now he's ready to do it again. This man who has grown up with me, side by side, through the awkward stages and the heart-breaks, through highs and lows and everything in between. Yeah, he's ruining me for sure.

I nod, unable to form words because I might actually cry.

"Good," he whispers. "That's my goal. Ruin you for everyone else because you're mine. You always have been."

He goes back down, his beard rough against my skin. He licks, sucks, and bites every single inch of me like he's on a mission. A mission to make me come undone. A mission to cement those words. A mission to make me feel and fall even more for him.

"Fuck me," I whisper, because as good as this feels, I just want him everywhere. I want to be filled by him.

"I don't have a condom. I didn't think this would happen."

"I'm on the pill." *Zero chill, Daisy. You have zero chill.*

He nods. "I don't want to push you to do something uncomfortable. I haven't been with anyone in years, and I got tested after my last relationship."

"Years?" Oh shit, I said that aloud.

"Mm-hmm. Turns out, the girl I knew I loved was finally single, and I wasn't going to risk missing my chance again. Even if it took me two years to show her."

I gasp. "Mateo, what are you saying?" Why are we having this damn conversation right now, when I'm seconds away from orgasming and he's naked between my legs? Good grief, Daisy.

"You broke up with that jerk, and I wasn't letting my chance slip away again. I love you, Daisy. I'm pretty sure I always have."

"I'm negative too!" It's the only thing I can think of right now. This is too much. Too many emotions. "No STDs, I mean. I got tested. I'm… We can… Fuck. I mean—"

"Shhh," he chuckles. "If you're sure, I would love nothing more."

"Please," I whisper again.

He lowers his face to my pussy, spitting on me, once, twice, then shoving two spit-covered fingers inside me.

"Fuuuuuuck," I groan, and his deep chuckle echoes, landing right in my core. I'm not going to last. I just know it.

His torso hovers over me, his face mere inches away from my face, and his lips kiss mine, gentle and tender. He slides in slowly, allowing me time to adjust to him. "You're so big," I whisper.

"The right size for you. You'll see."

He kisses me again, breathing steadily and marking the pace. He slides deeper, and I moan against his mouth, arching my back and wrapping a leg around him. There's so much space between us. I want his chest on mine. I want to feel him everywhere. All at once. Encompassing. Mine.

I pull him closer to me, and he lands on his forearms. His eyes search mine for something I can't quite name, but I want him to know I'm here, that I'm his. I want him to fuck me until there's not doubt in his mind. I roll my hips, and he drives all the way in.

I let out a sigh and bite my lips, not caring about where we are, lying on this cold ass floor, because in this moment, all that matters is that the man of my dreams is buried deep inside me.

"See? Perfect. I was made for you."

He picks up the pace, eyes never wavering. He's so controlled while I feel like I'm losing mine by the second. He holds my head with his hands, his pace moving faster, and with every stroke, he hits the right spot, as if this is nothing new, as if his body was meant for my pleasure.

He holds himself up with one hand while the other holds my leg and pushes it back towards my head, angling himself deeper.

"Fuck, fuck, fuck. I'm gonna come." Did I say that out loud?

My hands put pressure on his back, nails scratching, back arching, knees bending.

"Yes, come for me, baby." I sure as hell did.

"Get out of your head, Daisy. I wish you could see how beautiful you look when you're about to come. But I want you to make me feel it too." His pace picks up, and he moans when my pussy squeezes his dick.

"Stop moaning like that, or I'm—"

He does it again. He moans louder, and when he reaches the spot again and he smiles at me, I have no choice but to come. Fast and hard and, oh my God, all around him.

"Squeeze my dick, baby, Just like that." He closes his eyes, taking it all in. "Fuck, you're so pretty." He praises me over and over again, hitting the spot and not dropping my gaze. This is so intense. So beautiful. So perfect.

"You're going to make me come again," he whispers.

I wish I had the energy to say anything, but I don't, and he doesn't need it. One more pump and another scratch of my nails, and he spills inside me, warm and perfect as his breathing evens out and he slows his pace.

I moan softly, closing my eyes and dropping my leg wrapped around him. He slows his pace to almost nothing and drops his head next to mine. His face is nuzzled in my neck while our breathing syncs like it's natural.

"I love you," I whisper against his ear, and he tenses.

"I was hoping you did," he whispers against my neck.

"I love you in all ways, but I love you like this too," I coo.

He chuckles. "Good, because there's no going back. I can't have you like this once and never again. He kisses my cheek and slides out of me, leaving warm cum between my legs. "You ruined me too, by the way."

He gets up, offering me his hand. I look around at the mess we made, the trail of clothes and sand, the mark of our bodies on the floor, and I immediately feel the heat rushing up my cheeks again.

"Don't." He shakes his head. "That's why I said here and not in bed. The bed will be there tomorrow. This... this needed to be filthy, sloppy, and perfect." He lowers a peck to my lips. "It was perfect."

I nod, and he holds my hand, walking us both to the shower. The steam bellows quickly, and he steps us both inside.

Just as meticulously as he licked me, he does the same cleaning and washing my body. There isn't a spot that doesn't get touched by his fingers, not a strand of hair that he doesn't massage with the shampoo and then the conditioner. He holds me in his arms as we rinse, almost as if he's cashing a raincheck for not being able to touch me like this for years. He even scrubs and washes between my belly and pussy, under the small rolls that have formed through the years like it's nothing new for him. He touches me like he loves every inch of my body and he doesn't want there to be any doubt at all.

We step out of the shower, and he wraps me in two soft towels, covering my whole body. He squats next to me, picking me up newlywed style, and walks me to the bed. Our bed. *Who's smug now, bed?* I ask myself, shaking my head and smiling softly.

"What?" he asks.

"One bed, and we didn't even use it."

"The weekend is not over. You, however, need to rest. And I would love nothing more than to rest by your side." He lowers me to the bed and lifts the blanket to guide me in.

"I can't go to bed with my hair wet or I'll get a headache," I say. His eyes show amusement and a question he doesn't dare to ask.

"Don't look at me like that. It's true."

"Did my mother tell you that? One of her old wives' tales?"

I shrug. "Whoever it was, it's true. But you can go to bed if you want."

He gets up quickly, wrapping the towel around his hips and walking to the bathroom. In no time, he's back by my side, a blow dryer in hand. He plugs it in and proceeds to dry my hair.

"I can do it."

"Just because you can doesn't mean you should. I got it." He rakes his fingers through my hair as he dries it, massaging gently and making sure it's completely dry before he stops. He lays me down on the pillow like I'm a delicate princess, removes the towel, turns the lights off, and drops to the bed behind me.

"All dry." He kisses my cheek before retreating to his side of the bed.

"You don't strike me as a non-cuddler," I say, a little disappointed at the lack of warmth from his body on mine.

"I'm a cuddler." His voice is laced with joy. "Are you?"

"I'm willing to find out," I add, and he scoots closer, draping an arm around me, holding my breast and fitting perfectly behind me.

"Good night, Teo," I whisper.

"Good night, dream girl." I close my eyes and let today replay in my head. How do I keep him like this forever?

11

Intimacy That Only
Lovers Know
DELICATE BY DAMIEN RICE

Daisy

The distant memory of Mateo telling me he was going on a run and grab coffee wakes me from my sleep. The bed is empty, so it tracks, but fuck, I wish he was still here. The clock on the bedside table reads eleven, and I'm— ELEVEN O'CLOCK? I slept all morning? Did *he* sleep all morning? I know they're all early risers, but this is late, even for me. I sit up, groaning at the pain in every part of my body—perfect, delicious pain that reminds me of last night.

The kiss, the other kiss, the licking sesh, the absolute wild sex, the—oh my God, the cum play and Mateo's dirty talk. That man and his mouth. That man and his lips. That man and his words.

"Ugh." The groan slips past my lips effortlessly, a mix of thankfulness for yesterday and absolute terror at what might happen next. We said we loved each other while his tongue was between my legs, his mouth cleaning his cum from my pussy. What were we thinking? Was that the reality of our relationship? We've been in love with each other for years, afraid to say anything for fear of what? Falling? Ruining our relationship? Absolutely fucking everything up? Yup, sounds about right.

In reality, maybe I should've always known. Maybe I should've seen it. If I wasn't stupidly blinded by my own fears and thoughts, if I'd talked to him like an adult… Still, there's so much I want to know, so many questions, but I guess it'll have to wait.

I throw some clothes on—loose shorts and Mateo's shirt. I steal his shirts all the time, so it's not like it's new now. I always wondered if his ex-girlfriends cared when I would walk around wearing them, but he never seemed to, so I didn't bring it up. Now…what? Now I get to wear them as what? His possible girlfriend?

The never-ending questions won't leave me alone. I need fresh air, so I step out of the room in search of Mateo. If he hasn't come to me, maybe I'll go to him. The minute I step into the main hallway, I'm surprised by a group of people singing in Spanish, walking around with sleighbells, that instrument I love—a güira or something like that—tambourines, and drums in their hands.

I step away to let them pass, but one of the resort employees pulls me into the group and hands me a musical triangle, encouraging me to follow along. Well fuck, okay. Are they…caroling? Is this caroling? They keep walking, singing and dancing, so I follow along, trying to find the rhythm they all seem to share effortlessly.

We walk up the corridor to the main building. Every patron who shows up gets bamboozled into joining, so I don't feel nearly as bad. People who join seem to know the cheerful tunes, so I'm going to assume we're caroling. Dominican caroling, apparently. It's fun—or it would be, if not for the fact that I'm too worried about finding Mateo to really sing or hum or something.

I look to my right, and I think I see him, so I hand the triangle to one of the employees, shout a quick adios, and speed-walk to the narrow alley where I spotted Mateo. He's wearing his running clothes, so he definitely did say he was going for a run and getting coffee, but why did it take him so long? I guess I'm just assuming it's been long, since I actually don't know when he said that.

His body language is tense. Even though I can only see half of him, I can tell whoever he's talking to has him on edge. There's a wall between me and this person, Mateo's giant body covering them too.

"Please don't," Violeta says loud and clear as Mateo's finger runs down her cheek. The fuck? "I can't do this," she says on a small sob. I know I'm invading a moment of privacy, but what on Earth is she talking about?

"You sure can," Mateo whispers. He holds her with an intimacy only lovers know, the exact same way she seems to smile at him. What is going on here?

Violeta opens her mouth to say something, and I step closer, and—fucking hell, really? The damn carolers are right behind me, and I can't hear. I step closer, but so do the carolers, and oh no. That means... My words trail off at the same time Mateo turns, and Violeta's eyes snap wide when she sees me.

Mateo looks puzzled at first, and then he smiles. My gaze drops to their hands, and then his face turns as shocked as Violeta's. I knew it. I fucking knew it.

That's when I turn and run.

"Daze, wait!" Mateo shouts, but I don't stop to hear him out. I run, leaving the cheerful Christmas songs and my dignity behind. Of course he didn't want to come watch her get married. He still has feelings for her. Of course she was an absolute terror to me. She still has feel-ings for him. What a disaster. Me and my stupid feelings. I was convenient; he just needed to let some steam out with on the eve of his ex-girlfriend, almost fianceé, getting married.

I was so naive.

I enter the room, not daring to look back and see if Mateo followed me, and step in the shower. If he comes to find me, at least he won't see the tears. At least he'll think it's only water. I can play this off. I'm sure I can.

12

Wrong House, Wrong Person
IT WAS ALWAYS YOU BY MAROON 5 & BIRDS OF A FEATHER BY BILLIE EILISH

Mateo

Soft snores caress my throat, and it takes me a second to realize where I am and what's happening. It takes me longer to realize I'm awake and this is not a dream. Daisy in my arms is not a dream but a reality. A naked Daisy, at that. A sound asleep and completely spent Daisy. *I* had the night of my life. I can just hope she did too.

It's time for me to get up. My body will hurt forever if I don't, but I can't seem to move. How am I supposed to when I finally have *the* girl in my arms? As if she can hear my thoughts, she turns over, mumbling indecipherable words and hugging the pillow instead of me. I get up, get changed, and kiss her forehead.

"I'm going for a run."

"Don't go, or I'll think it was a dream," she whispers with her eyes still closed. We're more in sync than I thought.

I brush her hair back. "It wasn't. I'm here. I'll bring coffee. Sleep."

"You said you loved me." Her voice is groggy, full of sleep, and her brows are furrowed. Did she not believe me?

"I did, and I do." My fingers crawl through her hair. "I love you, in case you need to hear it again," I whisper. Her plump lips are parted slightly and soft breath escapes. I let out a sigh, kiss her forehead again and leave.

A ten minute run turns into thirty and before I know it I've been running for an hour and a half. Something about running that makes me feel like I can do anything. The first mile feels never ending but after I push through the discomfort, it makes me feel unstoppable. I do have to stop. The wedding is tonight and I want to spend the afternoon talking to Daisy.

I walk up to the resort, leaving the beach behind me and step up to the bar to order some coffee. Just my luck that Violeta is sitting there too.

"How's the bride feeling today?" I ask. She immediately looks my way with pure hatred behind her eyes.

"So how long did you cheat on me?" Violeta asks loud and clear. So this is why she's been acting upset all trip.

"I didn't cheat on you, Violeta. Ever," I reply.

"It's clear you did. How many times did we argue over Daisy? Too many to count, but I was right, huh? I mean look at you two. It's clear you've been a thing forever." She gets up, puts her drink down and speedwalks to the lobby. Chasing Violeta on her wedding day is not what I expected today.

"Stop walking so we can talk." So irrational, always.

She turns around and crosses her arms over her chest. This is a more secluded part of the resort, at the end of a corridor so at least we'll get some privacy.

"How. Long?!"

"You will not yell at me. I understand that you're furious for whatever reason but you will speak to me in the same way I've always spoken to you. I don't owe you anything but I'm willing to talk, emphasis on the word talk." She's erratic and it was one of our biggest issues when we dated. I never knew when she would be calm or when she would accuse me of shit I never did. It's a miracle I tolerated it for as long as I did.

"Fine! How long did you cheat on me?"

"Never. Not once. The day I realized I loved someone else, I broke up with you."

"You said there was nobody else and that we were just not meant to be," she adds.

"And both of those things were true. I didn't even tell Daisy how I felt about her until later. Hell, I didn't even realize it myself until—" I stop talking. Because nobody knows what actually happened. Well, Livie does. I thought it was time to settle down. I thought it was time to think about children and Violeta pushed for marriage and a family so much I thought it was me with the problem. I bought the ring but the day I was going to propose I realized it wasn't her hand I wanted to be holding when I was old, it was someone else's. So instead I broke up with Violeta. Livie knew I had bought the ring so I had to tell her what happened, minus the whole I'm in love with someone else thing.

Daisy also knew I bought the ring, so when I told her about not being together anymore, she assumed Violeta said no, and I just never corrected her. Wrong of me, but better than to let her know how I felt about her. Now it doesn't seem so silly, does it?

"Until when?" she asks.

I don't want to hurt her. I may not love her, but I did care about her, and she doesn't deserve to hurt over something she had no control over. My heart belonged to someone else. There was nothing she could do.

"Until the day we broke up. I promise, it had nothing to do with you, Violeta. But what I want to know is why you're holding a grudge. You're about to get married, to my cousin at that."

She shakes her head, and a tear falls down her cheek. "I'm just so hormonal. It did piss me off seeing you two together, but just because I thought you were cheating on me. I didn't want to be the joke."

"You're not a joke. We just weren't right for each other."

"Yeah, and this freaking pregnancy has me all unbalanced. I'm blowing everything out of proportion. I've treated everyone so poorly."

"Pregnancy?" I ask, and her eyes open wide.

"Oh, shit."

I chuckle. "Congratulations?"

"Thanks. Nobody's supposed to know. Jaime doesn't want to disappoint his parents, and I'm just...well, emotional."

"That's normal, but stop taking it out on others. It's not Daisy's fault. I promise you, she did nothing wrong. I'm happy for you, though. You always wanted to be a mom."

She nods and lets out a quiet sob. "I'm sorry." I step forward but hold myself back. I can't really console her right now, not when she's been so upset about my relationship with Daisy. I don't want her to get the wrong idea.

"Please don't," Violeta says loudly, and I nod. I won't

hug her, but at least I can wipe away her mascara-filled tears.

"I can't do this," she says between a small sob and holding her belly. She can, and she just needs to talk to Jaime.

"You sure can." I hold her hand reassuringly.

Violeta opens her mouth to say something, but her eyes dart to a ruckus behind me. I turn, and at first, I notice the group of carolers carrying a Christmas tune, but then I see Daisy. I smile immediately, but it's not returned.

She looks worried, and when I follow her gaze to me and Violeta holding hands, I can only imagine what she's thinking. Of course, she's going to think the worst.

"Daze, wait!" I shout, but she's already running back to the room.

"I gotta go," I tell Violeta, and she nods.

"Sorry I've been anything but pleasant. I'll get it together."

"Just leave my girl out of it. Go, enjoy your day. See you tonight, Mrs. Sanz."

"I always thought I would be… It just—"

"Wasn't me," I interrupt. "It's a good thing, Violeta. Jaime loves you, and I'm sure you love him back." She nods. "Then forget the past. Rest easy that it wasn't you, it was me. Go be happy."

She nods again.

"I do have to go, okay?" I squeeze her hand again and run back to catch Daisy. She's already gone, and judging by the way she took off, she's back in the room.

Why would she think the worst of me? I'm her best friend, but also…last night was a lot, and we didn't talk. Today, she probably woke up by herself and the first thing she saw was me holding Violeta's hand. Damn, I would think the worst too.

I open the door and hear the shower running. Okay, she is here.

I can see why she'd jump to the worst case scenario. Our hands together and maybe even the words I was saying—how much did she hear? What did it look like? It sure as hell probably looked like exes reconciling.

"Daze." I knock on the door.

"It's fine, Mateo. We got carried away last night. It's fine."

The water is loud crashing over her body. The swish of her scrubbing distracts me from what I'm here for: her. "It's not fine, and we didn't. Nothing we did last night was fine. Can I come in?" I ask.

"No, I don't want to talk," she shouts over the shower.

"Is this one of those instances when you tell me no but it's really a yes? Can I please come in? I want to be respectful but I also want to talk to you."

"I said I don't want to talk."

"You know what, Daisy? Sometimes, you're so infuriating." I drag my hand over my face in exasperation. My heart is racing, but I can't let it go. She needs to hear me. "I'm coming in." The bathroom is foggy, completely full of steam from the scalding shower. "Are you in pain?" I ask, because maybe I was too rough on her last night, and she's soothing her muscles with the heat of the shower.

She lets out an exasperated sigh. "No, I'm not in pain, Mateo, but I still don't want to talk."

"Good. Then listen." I pause, letting her know I mean it. Rarely do I tell Daisy what to do or what I think she should do, but right now, I need her to listen.

"I don't know what you think you saw, but Violeta and I were just talking. She thought I cheated on her with you, apparently has thought it all along, and she's emotional for many reasons. I did not go to her this morning."

She yanks the shower curtain aside, and suddenly, I'm face-to-face with a very pissed—no, not pissed, more like sad—but still breathtakingly naked Daisy. Waterdrops race down her skin like liquid gems, but her eyes are sharper than knives—cutting right through me.

"Why would she think that? And why was she emotional after being the one to call things off?" Her voice cracks, allowing me to see inside her feelings.

Now's the time, I guess. I lean back against the wall, exhaling hard, my palm dragging over my face. The short, rough bristles of my stubble scrape my fingers, a reminder of how she tasted last night. It's etched into me now—carved into memory, not just remembered but branded—and I'm not hoping, no, praying we get to do it again.

I'm trying my damnedest not to let my gaze wander, but it's impossible. Every curve sings my name. Each slope of her body is a road with no return. I've always known it, but last night made it undeniable: I fucking love her body.

"Focus!" she snaps, her fingers cutting the air like a whip and pulling a smile from my lips.

"Sorry. Sorry." I raise both hands in surrender, but my chest pounds. "Don't be mad at me, but…Violeta didn't break things off. I did." The confession comes easier than I thought—less like ripping skin, more like shedding dead weight, like I can finally breathe.

Her brows knit together, confusion clouding her face… confusion I placed there with my little white lies. "Wh-what do you mean? You bought the ring."

I nod slowly. "I know. Then I looked at the ring…and at the woman I bought it for…and I couldn't do it. I drove all the way to her house, ready to take her to the dinner I reserved for us, and I froze. I stood on her doorstep, staring at her—beautiful, yes, but not the woman I loved.

The ring was wrong. The house was wrong. The life

was wrong. But my heart?" I press my fist against my chest. "My heart was right. I just had to finally listen."

A shiver rolls visibly through her body, goosebumps prickling her wet skin. I step forward, twisting the faucet off, then grab her bathrobe. Draping it over her shoulders, I smile softly.

"Come on." She slips her arms into the robe, following my unspoken command, and I guide her out, leading us into the bedroom. I sit on the edge of the bed, motioning for her to join me.

"Daisy…" My voice roughens, but if there's a time when I need her to know I'm serious is now. "I told you last night. I love you. I always have. I just wasn't brave enough —or honest enough, with myself or with you—to admit it."

"You…you still feel that way?" Her voice trembles, and tears shimmer at the edges of her mossy green eyes, threatening to spill. I hope they're joyful tears and not sadness. I don't think I can bear it. I don't think I can bear her being upset or sad over something I did.

"What part of *I've always loved you* do you not understand? Come on, Daze. It's not that complicated." I brush my thumb across her cheek, tender, but she flinches, recoiling as if my touch harms her.

"Well, maybe the part of me that never knew. That part just watched you all cozied up with your ex."

"An ex I left because I realized I never loved her." My voice sharpens then softens, pleading. I don't want to scare her. I want her to understand. "You know the difference between a sensual touch and a friendly one. Which do you think that was?"

She only shrugs, defensive walls rising, completely getting into her irrational but beautiful brain. I've seen it before, when she doesn't want to admit defeat, but it's still infuriating all the same.

"You know…" I sigh, shaking my head. "For someone as brilliant as you, you sure can act oblivious sometimes."

Her brows snap together. "Are you calling me ignorant?"

"No." I lean closer, determined. "I'm saying you're letting your emotions fog your judgment. And I'm here, trying to tell you—it was never her. Never anybody else."

My nose flares as I try to contain my emotions. "They were not *you* so it was always going to be wrong."

Daisy's eyes bounce between mine, and her hands intertwine.

"It was always you. I was just too blind, too damn stubborn, to see it."

Her voice is small when she whispers, "So you two were not…" She trails off, her eyes dropping to her knees.

"No." I pause then force myself to continue. "I was actually asking her why she treated you so harshly for no reason. And she started crying because—" I hesitate. I hope Violeta forgives me for telling her secret, but this isn't just anybody. This is the love of my life. "Because she's pregnant. Emotional. Scared."

Her head snaps up, her green eyes wide. "She's pregnant?" A second passes, and then she mutters *finally* under her breath. We both laugh, the tension finally breaking. Everyone knows Violeta has always wanted kids.

"She'll be fine," I assure her. "And I hope she apologizes, because you didn't deserve that."

"It's okay. She doesn't have to."

"No, Daze. You didn't deserve the hurt she caused. She knows that now. I just hope she actually does the right thing."

"She's pregnant, Mateo! Her hormones are everywhere

—cut her some slack," she says, her heart so big, it nearly bursts from her chest. God, another reason I love her.

"Can we stop talking about my ex now?" I grip her hands, grounding us both. "I'd rather focus on what actually matters." I hold her gaze, memorizing the moment—tucking it away for the day our children ask when I first told their mother she was the love of my life, or for when we're old and gray and this memory is one of the few still clear. I hope it stays that way forever.

"What is that?" She bites her lower lip, eyes searching mine with desperate hunger for answers, answers I hope are as clear as my love for her.

"You," I say simply. "I want to talk about my feelings for you."

She hisses softly, breath catching as I lace my fingers with hers. "I told you last night, but I also told you a lot of things. I've been afraid." My voice is steady, but it's raw, laced with every single year I kept my feelings hidden. "But I love you, Daisy. I just don't want to lose your friendship. I'd rather have any piece of you than none at all. So, if you got carried away last night, that's fine. I won't be able to forget it happened," I swallow hard, "but I won't bring it up again. I just—"

She closes the space and kisses me, her legs falling on each side of me as she comfortably sits on my lap. *Yes, ma'am.* Her hands explore my hair while mine grab her ass. Oh shit, her ass. No, we're not doing this.

"Hold on, baby," I whisper against her lips. Her red and swollen lips. I can't believe I just stopped her from kissing me again.

"I need you to tell me with words, Daisy. I know you like my body, I know you liked what we did, but I need to know how you feel. I need to know what I'm getting myself into. I know I said I would take any part of you I can get, and that's still true, but I need to know before I do. Is this a carnal thing, or is this a heart and possibly forever thing?" Great job at scaring her, Mateo.

"Forever?" Her hands are still in my hair, and I bring my hands to her back. This is it. Tell her, you idiot.

"I…think so? I'm not proposing, not yet, but I am saying that's how I feel about you. That's how I've always felt. When I think of myself being old and grumpy, I think of you by my side. Always have."

"When did you become so chatty?" Her question is flirty and joyful, tittering between honest and deterring from the topic.

"Stop deflecting, Daisy. I'm serious."

She drops a peck on my lips. "I'm sorry, I'm just teasing. I would like someone to pinch me right now and remind me this is actually real."

I pull her lip between mine and bite gently. 'Real enough?" I ask with a wicked smile, hoping she can see I'm being honest and serious, but I'm still me, and this is still us.

"So what if I tell you I've had a crush on you since I was, like, six? My mom actually yelled at me for talking about kissing boys at that age. I'm never going to forget when I told her it wasn't boys I wanted to kiss. It was only you. And then, the older we got, that crush turned into more." She pauses and blinks harshly, letting out a breath, mustering courage to continue while I'm completely in shock. "And it's scary, so scary loving your best friend this deeply when you think he won't ever love you back the same."

"Daze," I interrupt.

"So, I'm sorry if hearing you say you feel the same seems completely out of the realm of possibility."

"Daze," I whisper again.

"I love you so much and so deeply, Teo, that I would fake date you even feeling the way I do to get your family to leave you alone over being at this wedding. Let that sink in."

I smile, and she chuckles. We both do. Her face falls on my shoulder. "I thought for sure I was gonna die when I saw I had to share a bed with the man of my dreams."

"That's what I call you."

She sits up, hands holding my face and her eyes bouncing left and right to mine.

"What?" Her voice carries confusion and joy. Oh, she's enjoying this, isn't she?

"The girl of my dreams. Because every time I close my eyes, it's only you I see."

"Are you always this much of a lover boy?" she asks.

"I can be whatever you want me to be, Daisy girl. Just be mine, yeah?" She doesn't answer my rhetorical question. She doesn't have to, because what she does instead lets me know everything I need to know. The way she kisses me, the way she pulls me as close as I can be, the way her chest is flushed against mine, all lets me know I don't only have her, but she has me too.

She loves me too.

The day has flown by, at least the afternoon, and now, it's time for the wedding. A wedding I had been dreading to attend, but I'm now actually looking forward to enjoying. Maybe my family can finally leave me and Violeta in the past and start focusing on her future with Jaime—

and mine with Daisy.

The wedding has been in full swing: a beautiful ceremony by the beach followed by a lively reception in an outdoor event pad. The beach frames the beautiful setting, but the music drowns out the crashing waves, and the fairy lights cast a glow over the space, the night sky forgotten.

Dinner was traditional Dominican Noche Buena food —plates full of telera, pastel en hoja, moro, and pork. Daisy's face lit up the moment she realized what we were eating. That's the beauty of traditions—you know what's coming, and both your head and your heart get excited for it. There are no surprises, just comfort. One spoonful, and suddenly, your body remembers joy, family, and hope on a day meant to embody all of that.

I'm sure there are details about tonight I should try to hold onto—the vows, the dresses, the decorations—but I don't. The only thing in my mind is how perfect this Christmas Eve has been now that I've told Daisy how much I love her—and she's told me the same.

So much for the last rule I'd set for myself: to keep my feelings hidden so I wouldn't change our friendship. I'm glad I broke it. I hope it changes everything for the better. I know, no matter what, Daisy will always be my best friend —but now I can't wait to grow old with her.

"So…how did the fake dating go? You get to go home tomorrow and what? You're going to pretend you don't love her?" Livie asks knowingly.

"How do you know I love her?" I ask, my attention never leaving my girl, who's dancing the night away with my little cousins.

"Anyone with two eyes can see there's only one girl for you, big bro. You just needed to be brave enough to actually utter the words." She pats my back. "I'm glad you finally did. I've never seen you smile as much as you did this weekend. And happy looks good on her too."

I look at Livie and smile. "Thanks, hermanita. Not everyone can meet the love of their life and immediately be honest about their feelings, you know? Some of us need a little push." I shove her gently with my shoulder.

"Mmm, actually, Alex and I fake dated too," she replies.

What?

"What?" I ask, and she giggles.

"It's a long story, but yeah. Crazy, huh?"

The song changes from a perico ripiao to a bachata, and I know exactly what to do. Daisy seems to think the same, since her eyes find me immediately.

"Oh my God, get a room!" Livie shouts.

"I'm not even close to her," I tell my little sister, now walking away from me in her frilly cupcake dress, as she calls them, to sit on her giant husband's lap.

"You don't need to be. It's all in the eyes, remember? Now go. Get out of here." She sends me away with her hand. I don't have to think twice about it. I walk up to my future and hold her in my arms.

"Hi, baby," I whisper.

"Oh, how I love the sound of that," she replies, her head falling to my chest while my hands rest on her exposed lower back.

"Get used to it." I kiss the top of her head and carry us along as the song fades into the distance like everything else does. Because when Daisy is in my arms, nothing else matters. Nothing else exists. Just me and her.

13

Meant To Be

FIN DE SEMANA (VERSION NAVIDEÑA) BY LOS HERMANOS ROSARIO & A NONSENSE CHRISTMAS BY SABRINA CARPENTER

Daisy

"I always knew you two were meant to be," Ada says, startling me.

"Oh, hi. You scared me." I tuck a piece of hair behind my ear and look around to see if anyone else is here.

"I'm sorry. I didn't mean to."

I nod nervously. Omar, Mateo's dad, is the warm and fuzzy one, the one who likes to converse and dance, the one I'm closer with. Ada... I don't know. I've never been able to figure it out. She is harsh on her kids, but she also is relaxed with other things. So her going out of her way to talk to me is...interesting.

"How did you know?" I ask now that I remember she said something.

She smiles looking at her son and daughter, who are dancing salsa on the floor. "A mother always knows. It's beyond the way he looks at you. It's the way he talks about you and how miserable he was every time you two were idiots and didn't date each other."

I gasp. "Ada, you know how to use that language?" I pretend to clutch my pearls.

"Ay, mija. Please. I know how, I just don't. Could you imagine if I used language like that in front of Olivia? She—"

"Would have turned out as perfect as she is now," I interrupt, because I don't want her to get the idea she can talk shit about Livie with me.

"Oh, no. That's not what I meant." She swallows hard. "I know I have not always been fair to O—" she clears her throat, "Livie, but I'm trying. What I meant was that she already uses explicit language without my aid."

"That she does." We both laugh, but I'm still unsure of her motive.

"I just came to say that I'm glad. You belong together. In forty years, those might be your kids dancing the night away." She points at Livie and Teo using her lips, the way all of them do. "You've always been a Sanz, mija. Now I'm glad we get to keep you." She stands, squeezing my shoulder, and walks away, leaving me alone with a smile.

The wedding is still going strong, but Mateo and I left. His family didn't even bat an eye, and it feels good to be away from the joyful chaos and back to being with just him. We went on a beach walk in the dark and just held hands while we talked. He stopped to kiss me more than once, and I swooned every time. We're heading back to the room, and I'm buzzing with anticipation.

I'm so deliciously sore from last night that maybe it's a

bad idea, but I just can't stop thinking about it. I can't stop thinking about how he took care of me and how much I loved every minute of it.

"Can I ask what you and Violeta were talking about?" Mateo asks, leading the way back to our room but keeping his tone friendly, a clear indicator if I say no, he won't be upset. Another thing I love about him.

"She wanted to apologize for 'being a bitch to me,'" I say, making quotation marks in the air. Mateo's eyes open wide, and I smirk. "Those were her words, not mine. I swear." I cross my fingers and bring them to my lips.

"I believe you," he teases, draping his arm over my shoulder and tucking me under his arm. "I'm glad she apologized. You didn't deserve to be treated like that."

"I would be very upset if I lost you so I understand."

"The thing is, she never had me, Daze." I look up at him, and I really, really hope he's saying what I think he is. "You do," he adds.

I let out a sigh. Yup, I'm done for. How does he expect me to carry on when he says things like this? The door to the room opens with a beep as Mateo steps aside and lets me in. He shuts the door behind him and stands with his back against it.

"Hi," I whisper as soon as he does, and he smiles, the exact way I was hoping for, relaxed and happy and completely comfortable.

Me, on the other hand? Not so much. I can't wait to get out of this dress for number one, and number two, that man looks like a snack with his khaki pants and his chacabana, a breathable linen shirt that's considered formal beach wear here. Most, if not all, of the men in his family wore one to the wedding, but nobody looked as good as he does now. But when is that new?

"Hi," I say again, breaking the silence. He walks to me

in long, confident strides, and I let out a small yelp, making him chuckle this time.

"You already said that." He reaches for me, one hand on my lower back and the other on my face. I'm so damn glad he's holding me, because I would have liquified onto the ground by now. Gone. Puddle. Melted by Mateo's gaze. Melted by Mateo looking at me like *that*.

"I must have forgotten words. You evaporated them with your stare." I clearly lost my damn filter too. One look from this man, and I forget how to function. How did I make this far in life? Oh yeah, he didn't fuck me senseless before. In this room. Actually, in this exact spot where we're both standing.

"Did I now?" His fingers trail up my back, closer to the zipper, and I let out a sigh of relief.

"Eager for something, Daisy girl?" he asks, amusement lacing his tone.

"To be out of this dress, yes? So eager."

He lowers his mouth to my ear. "That's a shame. You look fucking stunning in it."

Shivers run up my back, and I'm sure he can feel the goosebumps under his fingertips. He drags those skilled fingers up until he reaches the top of the fabric and drags the zipper down, going lower and lower until the dress is open. I feel like I can breathe again, but I don't. I can't. Not when he smells this good, like a spicy and fucking hot apple cider. There's no other way to describe his scent other than comfort and spice, like somewhere you want to be forever because you know you'll have a good time no matter what.

"Relax for me, baby," he whispers, licking and kissing my neck.

"I can't. No neurons left. Don't know how." I clearly

also forgot what shame is, because I have absolutely none. What is he doing to me?

His deep chuckle reverberates through every inch of my body, and I squeal when he sucks on my neck. Did he? "Did you just give me a hickey?"

"You have no idea how long I've wanted to do that."

I smack his shoulder playfully. "Mateo Sanz, are you sixteen? What the hell?"

He looks at me, mirroring my own playfulness. "This beautiful hickey on your neck *is* for sixteen-year-old me."

"Oh yeah, yeah, when you were dating whatever fake ass blonde was your girlfriend of the year."

"First of all, I don't know why we're talking about other women when the one I've always wanted is in front of me, and I would like nothing more but to devour her whole." I gasp as his hand slides from my neck to my hair. "Second, did you ever notice all of them were the opposite of you? I tried to trick my brain into thinking that maybe, just maybe, I wasn't utterly in love with you. I failed, obviously."

I roll my eyes, and he narrows his. "It's true, but Daisy, let me ask for a favor."

"Anything," I moan as his fingers trail to my arms. Then, he's peeling the dress off me. I forgot. I forgot for a second my back is exposed, and shortly, my whole body will be. He drags the dress down my body, groaning when he sees what I'm wearing.

"Stop talking about the past. All I want is the right here and now with you, our future. Got it?" The dress is a pile of fabric on the floor. I've dared to look down, but my eyes don't go to the dress. They go to Mateo who's hands are wrapped around my thighs while his face is right in front of my center.

He slides his fingers on the hem of my lace panties and

groans again. "You've been walking around with this sexy as sin underwear all night?"

"Always, actually. I love feeling sexy, so I wear lingerie every day, and sometimes no bra, like yesterday." Today was different. The dress today required my breasts to look full, not like saggy potatoes, so I wore this matching set I love. The thong is mesh with little red bows on the waist and the bra—well, the bra is completely see through, with embroidered bows on the nipples.

"You look like a gift," he says before he closes his mouth over my pussy and sucks, panties first, and then my skin. Damn, I'm so ready for him, it's not even funny.

He kisses my belly, over my belly button, and when sees my breasts, he offers me another moan.

"Fucking hell, Daisy. If this is what you always wear, I'm going to have a really hard time keeping my hands to myself."

"I can get used to that," I say. He lowers his mouth over my nipple and bites it gently. There's too much in between us. Too much fabric. Too much space. Too much everything. I want him now.

"Teo." His name rolls off my tongue like a plea while he licks and sucks my nipple into his mouth.

"Mmm," he hums, and I feel it all the way down to my core, to my toes. I love how he can't seem to keep his mouth away from my body. He makes me feel so sexy and desired, and I don't think I'll ever come down from this high.

"Too much." They're the only words I'm able to mutter.

He stops instantly, as if my words are iced cold water. "Is this too much? Are you in pain from yesterday?"

"No, silly. Not *you're doing too much*. There's too much space between us. There are too many layers between us.

There are too many clothes on your body. All of that. I just didn't have any words."

The way he smiles at me makes my entire body hum.

"I can fix that," he adds, and in one quick swoop, he removes his shirt. Damn, he's hot. I all but strip him with my eyes, walking backwards to the bed.

"Sit," he commands, and I obey, landing on the edge of the bed. He removes the rest of his clothes, his eyes not leaving my body. My breathing cranks up at the pure hunger I see in them.

"Bra, off." I shiver at his tone and do as he says. Damn, bossy Mateo might be my favorite. My soft spoken, assertive, kind Mateo unravels at the sight of me, and I like it. I free my breasts, earning a guttural groan from him.

"I like how much you seem to like these," I tease, bringing my hands to my breasts and pinching my nipples.

"Do it again." I do as he says and roll my hips searching for friction. I want *his* touch, though, not mine.

He kneels in front of me, his hands traveling up my thighs to my underwear, pulling them down in one, quick swoop. I'm thankful he didn't rip these ones off. I really like them. He peppers kisses up my legs and my thighs, all the way up to my core, and I moan.

"You have the prettiest pussy, Daisy. It's so perfect." He slides his tongue over my folds, and I welcome it, bucking my hips against his face and feeling his rough beard right where I want it. He licks, one, twice, and spits on me. So filthy. So mine.

"I want your dick. Now," I gasp, and he chuckles.

"And you'll get it, but we went pretty rough last night, and I want to make sure you're okay."

"I can handle it," I say quickly. I don't want him to think I'm incapable of fucking two days in a row just because of my health conditions.

He chuckles as he softens his features, lifting his browns to meet mine. "I'm sure you can, but we have a lifetime, baby, and I want to make sure you can enjoy this."

I open my mouth to refute, but he beats me to it. "Without pain. I want to make you feel good and only good."

I pout. "Fine!" He lowers his head back to my center, licking the worries away. Damn, he's good at this.

"Get out of your head," he says before he blows on my clit and sucks it between his lips.

"Ah!" I gasp.

"Good. Relax." I do just that. I relax against him and just let the pleasure wrap me up whole. It starts in my toes and reaches my belly in no time. He slides a finger in then two, stretching me so nicely around them. I'm chasing the high like a skydiver preparing to jump, and I'm ready to fall.

He doesn't let me, though. As soon as he has me writhing and moving under him without restraint, he slides his fingers out of me and kisses up my body instead.

"I was almost there," I say, and he chuckles.

"I know, but you said you wanted my dick, no? Well, here you go." His hands rest next to my face, and his mouth crashes against mine as he finds my entrance and glides in slowly. He bites my lip, allowing me space to breathe while he grabs my leg and pushes it back, stretching me around him.

"You—"

"You feel so good." He beats me to it. It's like he knows what I'm thinking, what I'm feeling, before I have a chance to even form the thoughts. He knows how to read me so well.

He thrusts in and out of me, slowly at first, driving deeper and deeper. I bring a hand to press over my clit, and he smiles. "I love that you know what you need and go for it. Do you want me to take over?" I shake my head as I touch the spot I know will send me over the edge quickly.

"God, I love you. Always, but like this, about to burst for me, I love you even more."

"Teo," I whisper.

"Let go, Daze. Fall with me." He drives in and out, again and again, his eyes not leaving mine, dark and full of lust. I can't hold it anymore, and as the warm feeling builds behind my belly button, I let myself explode.

"Yes, there it is." Something flashes behind his eyes, and then I feel it. Warm liquid hits my inner walls contracting around his thickness, making me feel so full.

"Yes," I moan, and he nods. He slows his pace as we both come down from the euphoric high, one we climbed as two but reached as one.

"Damn." My voice is breathy, full of want and feelings. Feelings that have been buried deep down for so long. Feelings I know were reciprocated, and now, we get to share them all.

"Damn indeed," he says, his voice low and groggy and completely spent. He gives me a quick peck on the lips before collapsing next to me and opening his arm to get me to snuggle with him.

We're both sweaty and tired and full of love. Well, I'm full. He's empty, I guess. I chuckle at my own thoughts, but he just hums.

"I love you."

"I love you too, my Daisy girl. I love you too."

"Merry Christmas." It's in the distance. A soft voice. A quick reminder Christmas is here again. Another year, another morning I get to wake up with—wait…Mateo!

I open my eyes, and there he is, all smiley and fresh as a daisy. Cool as a cucumber. All of it, at once.

"Normal people don't look like that early in the morning." My voice is so drawn-out and husky.

His chuckle reminds me instantly of all the events of the trip, and I smile to myself.

"I have something for you," he says, piquing my interest.

"Oh yeah." With only one eye open, I take his hand and let him help me and sit up. I'm naked and tired from being bent over more ways than one, but I wouldn't have it any other way. I drag the blankets over my chest and wait to see what he has for me. In his hands lies a little perfectly wrapped gift.

"I didn't bring anything. I figured we'd just wait until we got back home."

Honestly, who brings a gift on a tropical vacation? Five days of sunscreen, sand, meddling family, and cocktails was enough for me to worry about, not showing my best friend how I felt about him. That doesn't exactly scream wrapping paper required. We fly home tomorrow. Gifts were supposed to wait until then. At least I thought so.

"Open it." His smile isn't just bright, it's blinding, and it simultaneously lights up the whole room.

I tug the green string, and cinnamon slams into my senses. It smells like their childhood kitchen, flour in the air, Mateo and Livie's laughs echoing off tile walls, his rising above all. Inside the wax paper sits a cinnamon-and-salt ornament, I know exactly what it is, since we used to make them as kids. His dad would always help, and through the years, the tradition just kind of went away.

I turn it carefully, the texture gritty against my fingertips. These things snap if you even look at them too hard. "How did this survive in your suitcase?" I ask, but the question sticks in my throat when I notice the details: two small thumbprints pressed into a heart, the words *Our First*

Christmas Together carved deep, with the years 2002 and 2025.

"Our first Christmas as kids," he says softly, "and our first as a couple."

My chest tightens. "When did you even make this?"

"This morning," he says casually, like it's normal to craft sentimental keepsakes before breakfast.

"You sleep like you're auditioning for a coma, and I wake up with the sun. I thought maybe it could be our tradition. I'll make you something while you rest, and then we spend the day together."

He's so thoughtful, so kind—so painfully correct about me and mornings. He's sunrise and salt air; I'm blackout curtains and coffee. And somehow, he makes us fit.

"And in this plan," I ask, narrowing my eyes with a grin tugging at my lips, "when do I get to do something for you?"

"Not that it's tit-for-tat," he teases, "but you're awake now, aren't you?"

Unbelievable. This man. I giggle and shake my head.

I set the ornament gently on the nightstand and throw myself at him. His chest is warm against mine as I hug him, hard enough to nearly knock us both flat. "Merry Christmas to you too. I love the ornament. And I love you." I kiss his cheek, quick and playful, then swing a leg over him until I'm straddling his hips.

"What now?" he asks, sinking back into the pillows, hands resting on my ass like he's already claimed his prize.

"Now," I murmur, leaning close enough to breathe in his scent, warm, spicy, and now a touch of cinnamon too, "we get to do the rest of our lives together. No rules." My heart is pounding, and I wonder if he can hear it too. "Well…maybe one final rule."

His eyebrows lift. "What's that?"

"That we keep being best friends, even now that we're lovers."

His smile softens, warm enough to melt me where I sit. "I wouldn't have it any other way."

I pause, memorizing everything: the crash of waves outside, the faint tang of salt clinging to my skin. The memories from not only last night, but the entire weekend, the way his eyes catch the light and hold me steady, his scent, his kindness, his eyes that never leave mine. The weekend has been magic, and I can already see Bee's jaw hitting the floor when I tell her every detail.

"Now, for your gift..." My voice drops as I tug the sheets over us, a grin playing at my lips.

I show him exactly how much I love him—without needing a single word.

Epilogue

Daisy

A year later

"Pass me the pasteles, mija," Omar, Mateo's dad, says. His voice is warm, a little gravelly, the kind of voice that makes even a simple request sound like an invitation to belong. I don't remember exactly when he changed my nickname from sweetheart to mija, but I take it like a badge I've secretly longed for.

I do as he says and smile softly at him, because getting to know him better this past year has been unexpectedly healing for me and my daddy issues.

He's an incredible dad—gentle but steady—and Mateo and Livie are lucky to have him. He's quiet most of the time, but he likes board games, and I do too. It feels like our own private language when we play. After the whole fake-to-actually-dating thing last Christmas, we've gotten closer, I guess now that he knows I'm not just the friend. Still, I would love to know when I can actually wear the 'mija' tag proudly. I hope I will one day, right?

I mean, I've been dating Mateo for a year now. We moved in together almost immediately after coming back from the Dominican. My lease was up, and he couldn't get me in his house fast enough. Our house, as he would correct me, gently but firmly. Did he let me put any money down? Nope. He still won't let me pay for anything. When I threw a fit about it, he asked for five dollars to pay the notary and added my name to the title. "Just sign here," he said, and it was all done.

Livie and I are closer than ever…but still, I'm just the girlfriend. I don't want to complain or sound ungrateful, because really, being his girlfriend is what I dreamed of for years. Now, though, I'm getting impatient. I just want him to put a ring on it. Call me superficial or cliché or whatever, but I want the ring. I already have the house and the man and the family—since they took me in as one of their own—and now, I want the ring.

"Here." I smile at Omar as I pass the plate, but his attention flickers toward Mateo, a crease of concern in his brow. I don't blame him—Mateo looks pale, like he's about to keel over.

"Hey, are you okay? Do you need water?" I ask, leaning in to touch Mateo's forehead instinctively. He feels fine, but he doesn't look it. He's barely touched his food, which is practically a crime in this house.

"Maybe he needs to go for a walk. Why don't you take him down to the river for some fresh air?" Ada, his mom, suggests gently.

Their house is a beautiful cottage-style home right in the heart of Magnolia Springs, with the spring-fed lake as their backyard. It's the kind of place pulled from the glossy page of a southern design magazine—cozy and a little magical. We pass the enclosed patio, stepping into the open air, the grassy yard sprawling wide under majestic oak trees. The branches stretch like arms above us, draped with white garden lights that sway softly in the breeze. It's straight out of a small-town-of-my-dreams movie.

Their backyard is goals, if I do say so myself. When we were little, Livie, Bee, and I used to pretend we'd get married right here in this very yard. We planned every detail—where we'd set up the decorations, the colors of the bridesmaids' dresses, even the exact square of grass where the dance floor would go. We believed it would be Livie's wedding venue, but she ended up getting married in Atlanta, somewhere more practical, where both her family and Alex's could get to easily. It was beautiful, of course, but still—every time I walk under these lights, I think of our girlish dreams.

We follow the path—or really, Mateo leads, and I trail behind, trying to catch up with his strange silence. He's so oddly quiet, and I don't understand what changed. He was fine this morning, before dinner, laughing with me in the car. Maybe it was the food? He did barely eat. It can't be work—he took time off again for the holidays.

"Teo, baby, wait!" I call out, my voice sharper than I intend. He's all the way to the dock and stops the second he hears me.

He turns, and my breath catches. *Holy shit.* He looks so devastatingly hot in the moonlight. Filthy thoughts flash through my head: I could one hundred percent strip him and suck him off right here. The image makes me flush, and I shake it off. Obviously, his parents are twenty yards away inside. Definitely not the vibe. I press out a shaky laugh and exhale.

The night is chilly, the kind of crisp that sneaks

through clothes. Despite my long-sleeve shirt and leggings —I'm choosing comfort these days, because the food here is too good to waste energy worrying about how my jeans or dress fit—the cold breeze prickles at my unshaved legs.

If looks could warm me, though, this one would. Mateo's looking at me like I'm both a breath of fresh air and a hot summer night, like I'm the beginning and end of every season. His eyes spark fire within me, burning away every trace of doubt. How did we get from I might throw up at any moment to this?

He extends his hand, palm up, and I take it without thinking, stepping closer into his spicy, familiar-scented space. This scent right here is engrained in my being, especially now that I fall asleep on his chest every night.

"Hi," I whisper.

"Daisy girl."

"Teo," I breathe, my voice trembling. He smiles like he's savoring the sound of me unraveling. "Are you feeling better?"

"Mm-hmm," he hums.

"Fresh air was all you needed, huh?"

"You."

"I—what?"

"You were all I needed."

The dock seems to tilt beneath me, my heart pounding so loud, I can hear it in my ears. His words sink deep, and I'm beyond confused. I laugh nervously, the sound breaking the night's stillness.

"That's…okay? I—we're together, you know?"

His smile widens, softer this time, almost boyish. "Yeah." He doesn't say anything else, almost like he's waiting for answers. He didn't ask a question, though, so I truly don't know what he wants, and it's dizzying.

"You asked me last year if Christmas was my favorite holiday, and I said no, remember?"

"Yeah, but you lied," I reply, and he nods.

"Do you know why it's my favorite holiday?" I shake my head and bite my lip. Where is this going?

"Because since I was seven years old, I got to spend them with you, every year. For over twenty years, I knew no matter what, it was Daisy Day."

He takes a deep, shaky breath, like he's been rehearsing this in his head all night and can't hold it in any longer. His hand squeezes mine once, and then he lowers himself to one knee, right there on the dock.

My hands fly to my mouth. "Oh my God."

The fairy lights above us glow brighter—or maybe it's just my vision blurring with tears. Fucking finally! I can't say that, can I? Nope, I should wait for him to speak, live in the moment. I should one hundred percent get out of my head.

Mateo's voice wavers, but his eyes never leave mine. "I wrote this a million times over because I was lost about what to say. You'd think a man who has been practicing how to ask the girl of his dreams to marry him for decades would know what to say, but the words failed me."

Well, shit. Now I'm crying.

"You already know I can't live without you. You're not just my girlfriend, Daisy. You're my family. My home. My best friend. My confidant. My partner. My brightest light on a dark day and the last person I want to see when I close my eyes. You are my everything, and I don't want to wait another day to make that official."

He pulls a small velvet box from his pocket, flipping it open with a hand that trembles only slightly. The ring catches the moonlight, glinting like every childhood wish I ever made under these very trees.

"Will you marry me?" he asks, and a sob breaks free from my lips. I don't know what to say or do; all I can do is cry with my hands covering my mouth.

"Well, say something," someone shouts from behind me, but I'm too afraid to turn around to see who it is. Then, it registers. Oh no, no, no. I didn't say anything!

"Yes! Oh my God, yes! All I've ever wanted was to say yes, Mateo."

He slides the prettiest gold ring on my finger, and I throw myself at him, tackling him to the damp grass. I kiss him gently at first and then ravenously, and I don't stop until he whispers against my lips, "Everyone's here."

I look at him puzzled. "Who's everyone?"

A mix of "Surprise!" and "Everyone!" shouts greet us, and I look around, the tears still flowing. All our friends, my sister, my mom, Mateo's family, and Livie and Alex are here, smiling so big at us.

"Fucking finally," Livie shouts, and we all laugh.

"Come on, lovebirds. Let's take this party inside. I'm cold!" my little sister whispers, and we follow her directions.

We spend the rest of the night intertwined, surrounded by our friends and family, and I thank myself again for breaking all those rules a year ago.

Want more Daisy and Mateo? Read the bonus epilogue here

The One Final Rule

Acknowledgments

Do you feel that? Do you feel the warmest hug around your heart after a busy day? A warm, fuzzy coat over your shoulders after a cold moment? How about a listening ear from your best friend you haven't seen in way too long? Yeah? Because that's exactly what I wanted you to feel when you finished this book.

I'm no stranger to writing humor and light-hearted characters, but after finishing *The Lies Always Told* in my Baker Oaks series (if you know you know), I didn't think I could write joy like this again. Thank you for sticking through with me with every type of story—the emotionally devastating ones and the light-hearted hug in the shape of a book ones too.

I have so many people to say thank you to, but I want to start with YOU, because without your love for my stories and your support, I wouldn't be here. This story would probably not exist if it wasn't for you, so thank you.

Thank you to my favorite and forever best friend, Joey. There's always some of you in all my main characters, and it's no different for this one. Thank you for being patient with my late morning wake ups and my chaotic thoughts.

To my alphas and betas, Maeghen, Mandy, Adriana, Colleen, Kristina, Lulu, Sam, Michelle, Jennifer, Anya: thank you for always jumping into reading my work even when it's last minute and incomplete. I love you all.

To my bestie author girl Hollie for always saying 'you can do it' when I'm completely delusional about timelines.

To Liss Montoya for thinking about this super fun project, and to Maria Rigou and Michelle Carrero for also being incredible at bringing The Holiday Rules series to fruition. This was so much fun!

To my kids, because you remind me to believe in magic every day. Thank you for your patience as Mami navigates all the things.

To my editing team, Jayné and Alexa: what would I even do without you? I'd have a very, very, very unfinished manuscript is what I would do. These stories are what they are because of you. Love you!

To Mayhara from Mayharate for the most beautiful illustration for the cover in the entire world. I'm forever obsessed with your work. You will never get rid of me, that's for sure.

To Cassie, my brand manager and PA… I don't even know what to say, because thank you isn't enough. I don't know what I would do without you and Cassie's Creative. Thank you. Thank you. Thank you.

To my content and arc teams: I love you all. That's all. Specially Brandy and Mckenna! Thank you for playing games and winning them too!

To my Patreon babes, especially Scarther and Nancy, thank you for supporting my author career in this huge way!

Thank you to Ms. Kim and Ms. Anna at 4th Street Deli for being incredible, and making the best broccoli salad ever.

And last but not least: thank you to Joey again. Thank you for being sunrises and salt air to my black out curtains and coffee. You make us fit just fine.

Now, off to cry in author tears and on to the next book.
143,
Ambar

Also by Ambar Cordova

The Baker Oaks Series

The Truth Never Spoken—a heartfelt second-chance romance where her sexy ex says she needs to go home with him after they have not seen each other in ten years.

The Trail Often Crossed—a fast-paced sports romance where the hot new-to-town tattoed man finds out the spitfire and afraid-to-love bartender from the night before is his new rival.

The Road Sometimes Taken - A best friend's brother to lovers, millionaire roadtrip romance.

The Lies Always Told—an angsty age gap, secret relationship romance! Available now!

ROM COMS

Once Upon A December Duology

The Gift Rarely Given—a hot and spicy Christmas novella where an ex-QB with a bad reputation proposes to fake date a confident plus-size Latina to help him fix his image and get her mom to stop setting up with bad dates.

More from The Holiday Rules:

The Twelve-Hour Rule By Maria Rigou : A strangers to lovers Christmas Novella.

The Christmas Cover Rule by Michelle Carrero: A strangers to lovers Fake Dating Christmas Novella.

The No Falling Rule by Liss Montoya: A millionaire, multicultural, strangers to lovers Christmas Novella.

About the Author
GRAB A BOOK, FALL IN LOVE, STAY A WHILE ♥

Ambar Cordova is a romance author of heartfelt multicultural stories. With a focus on raw, emotional story-telling, she creates relatable worlds with flawed characters that feel real. She grew up in the Dominican Republic and brings diversity and her latin experiences as inspiration to her stories. Ambar writes books that readers not only escape into, but also find themselves in.

Her debut series, Baker Oaks, features a cozy small town in Florida showing multicultural stories that bring butterflies and sometimes tears to her readers. When Ambar is not writing she's spending time with her family and reading in her she shed. Ambar enjoys boat rides, traveling, and spending time outside.